With her very first novel, *ABOVE SUSPICION*, Helen MacInnes entered the front rank of suspense writers—a position she has maintained for many years. For the reader who has not yet made the acquaintance of this superb storyteller, *HORIZON* will be a treat.

Helen MacInnes

HORIZON

FAWCETT CREST • NEW YORK

HORIZON

THIS BOOK CONTAINS THE COMPLETE TEXT OF THE
ORIGINAL HARDCOVER EDITION.

Published by Fawcett Crest Books, a unit of CBS Publications,
the Consumer Publishing Division of CBS Inc., by arrangement with Harcourt Brace Jovanovich

ISBN: 0-449-24012-6

Printed in the United States of America

22 21 20 19 18 17 16 15 14 13

For my brother Ian

We are but warriors for the working-day;
Our gayness and our gilt are all besmirch'd
With rainy marching in the painful field;
There's not a piece of feather in our host ...
And time hath worn us into slovenry:
But, by the mass, our hearts are in the trim.

—KING HENRY V

CHAPTER 1

When you rested on one elbow the third strand of wire cut across the mountaintops. When you sat up and stared at the gray faces of the precipices, irregular and massive against the high blue sky, it was the top strand of wire which now spoiled their line. However you looked you were always forced to remember you were caught, caged like an animal. The only way to see the mountains and enjoy them was to walk right up to the ten-foot wall of barbed wire and look between two of its strands. Even then, although you weren't actually looking at the barbs, you could feel them, twisted and jagged, trying to draw your eyes away from the mountain peaks. And then a sentry would yell some fine Italian curses at you, and if you didn't move quickly enough out of the twenty-foot zone behind the wire a bullet would whistle towards you. It depended on the Italian's temper whether it whistled high above or unpleasantly near your shoulder.

Peter Lennox's set face—grim, hard, expressionless—turned away from the view of mountains. He felt his tense body might give his thoughts away; he leaned back on his elbow again. His fingers touched a solitary tuft of grass-blades, pitifully small and yet growing in spite of the heavy boots which paced over this ground. You have a view, Lennox was thinking, but you cannot enjoy it. You've fresh air, coming down from the freedom of the mountains, but all you can smell is the tannery which lies between them and you. The smell seemed always ripest at this late afternoon hour, just at the time when the

9

prisoners were exercised. Perhaps that was why this period was chosen for their daily forty minutes of fresh air. (As a prisoner you had come to believe that anyway, whether it were true or not: it fitted in naturally with all the pettiness of malicious restrictions and unnecessary domination which had become the background to your life.) Lennox began counting the short blades of grass. . . . Nine. One more than yesterday. He began remembering how it felt to walk over a whole stretch of soft, fine grass. Hundreds and hundreds of blades—thousands, millions, of blades of grass. And here he could touch nine. He began admiring their defiance and their determination. And somehow his confidence—which had seemed to desert him this morning—began to return.

He turned his head carefully to look at the walls of the prison behind him. You could tell from their appearance that they were thick and clammy, enclosing small dank rooms behind the boarded-up windows. Once the place had been called a castle—it was set proudly enough on the mountainside above the valley. Then it had become a nunnery, with its upper rooms walled into many cells. Later still it had become a hospital for the poor and the despairing. It had been a natural choice for housing prisoners of war, where men who had tried unsuccessful escapes from other camps could be taught that hope was abandoned by all those who entered here.

Dispassionately Lennox studied the walls; the scabby plaster, once white and now weathered into green and brown streaks; the eternally shuttered windows. Only the windows in the left wing of the castle were not boarded up. That was where the Italian commandant and his staff had their quarters. They, too, suffered from the perpetually sweating walls. But at least they had heating when they needed it, and furniture and rugs and other aids to comfort. Lennox smiled grimly as he wondered where the commandant's friends were this afternoon. The windows were empty: no one there to stare down at the men below as at some monstrous wild animals in a zoo. The adjutant's windows were empty too. No girls laughing up there today. No gramophone records being played. Even the guardroom windows were silent, staring blindly at the mountains rising on the other side of the valley.

Lennox shifted his weight to his other elbow. Something's wrong, he thought; something's wrong with the Italians. It seemed as if the other prisoners felt that too, for they were enjoying their forty minutes of fresh air with a good deal more zest and noise than usual. The stretch of grass outside the barbed wire was empty of the customary spectators. Generally some civilians from the town would choose this time of day for their late afternoon stroll past the camp. There, on the wide slope of grass at the prescribed (and safe) distance from the barbed wire, some would stand, some would stare, and some would laugh. "Eighth Army!" was the usual gibe, spat out with a good deal of venom as an arm was raised to point—in the silly way in which a mocking child points—at the ragged men crowded into the meager exercise ground.

But today there was no one there, no one except scattered sentries. And the prisoners—at least, those who were fit enough—were enjoying themselves. Some thirty of them had gathered round the goal post—the solitary tree which never blossomed, but in some strange way still stood erect in a patch of bald earth—and were playing a game of mock football. There wasn't enough room for a proper game: the men had to content themselves with taking odd shots at the goal. The ball was a wad of old newspapers tied into shape with knotted string. (Last week the leather ball which the Red Cross provided had been confiscated, after it had "accidentally" smashed the adjutant's bedroom window, scattering his squealing guests with the broken pane.) The men had slipped off their tunics and were playing either in shirt sleeves or vests. The deep bite of the North African sun was still on their

skin. Their months of captivity, of work in the near-by
tannery, of fresh air and exercise measured by minutes
in the late afternoon, had only bleached the varieties of
brick red and walnut-brown into a sickly tan. Lennox
looked down at his hand, with its bones and sinews now
so prominent. A most sickly and unbecoming tan, he
decided. His wound didn't improve the general appearance: it had healed in an angry white gash across the
back of his hand. He began flexing his muscles, slowly
and carefully. The wound had healed, but every month
the hand seemed tighter. It might be merely worry or
imagination which tightened it. Once he got out of here
the hand would probably be strong once more.

About a hundred other men, less energetic than the
players, lounged on the hard patch of earth. They were
content to be spectators, content to catch the last rays of
autumn sunshine before they were herded behind the
thick walls for the long night. Besides, dysentery doesn't
encourage a man to chase after a football, or to plod
round and round a meager rectangle of restricted space
as a few of the more determinedly hearty were now doing.

From the scrambling group of players there was a
shout, "To me, lad, to me!" That was the sergeant major,
square-set, broad-voiced, and as Yorkshire as his vowels.
He was waiting impatiently for a pass from Miller, the
New Zealander. And Miller, swerving aside from two of
the walkers who doggedly kept their even pace in spite
of footballers and bodies strewn over the ground, obliged.
The sergeant major swung into position, and missed the
goal by a foot. There was a laugh, and a mock cheer.

Miller had dropped out of the game. He was limping
slightly, as if his wound was troubling him again. He
picked up his shapeless jersey, wiped his brow with it,
and pulled it over his cropped fair hair. He was walking
slowly, at a tangent, stopping here and there to speak
a word or reply to a question. Gradually he drew near
the waiting Lennox. The sentries guarding the double wall

of barbed wire would have thought there was only chance in the meeting of the two men. Lennox's tight mouth relaxed as he glanced over his shoulder once more and saw the commandant's and adjutant's windows were still quite lifeless. He felt in his pocket for a cigarette, and expertly halved it.

"Thanks," Miller said. "I've a match." He bent down to light Lennox's half. "Mountain gazing as usual, I see."

Lennox half smiled as he pulled steadily at the mutilated cigarette. His gray eyes flickered over the New Zealander's face and then returned to the wire. The sentries were still bored. The bell, which would end this reprieve in the open air, would not ring for another six minutes. It looked as if Miller and he could talk before they were shut away into their separate sections of the prison. Miller was pretending to watch the game of football. They were two men drawn together by a cigarette and a match, with no other interest at the moment except the game and a row of mountains. They seemed to be as bored as their guards.

The New Zealander was speaking, quietly, lips scarcely moving, head unturned. "Johann has come through."

Lennox's lips tightened on his quickly burning cigarette. "No," he said at last.

"Yes. Told you he was all right."

"The buttons?"

"Complete set. German infantry, as you wanted."

When Lennox didn't answer, Miller said quickly, "Johann's all right. I've told you. He's Austrian. Tyrolese. Hates the Eyties. Hates the Germans, who abandoned him and his people to Mussolini."

"You are taking a steep chance," Lennox said. Seven months of planning, of alarms and subterfuge. Seven months of tedious preparation of gathering a disguise together. Seven months of giving up most of his precious food packages to pay the more bribable guards, so that he could secure a piece of string or sewing thread or a small tube of glue. Seven months of worry and strain, of perpetual threat of discovery, of working out a map, of learning more German and enough Italian. And now the buttons, which would give the finishing touch to his old army coat, bleached and dyed so secretly and pains-takingly, had materialized. They came too easily. After so much trouble and worry they came much too easily. He stared at the wire, and it seemed to tighten round his throat.

Miller was still talking about Johann. "I told him noth-ing about you. He thinks the buttons are for me. So if he's been planted here to trap us he will give the wrong information." He allowed himself to glance at Lennox for a moment. This will be his third attempt, he remem-bered: the first from this camp, but the third altogether. The other two had failed because of sheer bad luck. Miller himself had only tried once, but it hadn't been planned in the careful way Lennox worked out his escapes. When a man planned like Lennox it was unfair that he shouldn't succeed. He remembered now that in each case Lennox had been caught (once in sight of Jugoslavia, once in Southern Italy) by trusting to the good faith of smiling civilians. No wonder that the men-tion of Johann, the seventeen-year-old Tyrolese in the prison's post office, had stiffened Lennox like that. He scarcely trusted his own shadow now. And you couldn't blame him: not after two disappointments.

"I passed the buttons to Jock Stewart when he was scrubbing the post office floor today," Miller went on quietly. "He is hiding them in your mattress now."

Lennox stirred. That at least was a good plan. Stewart, the intransigent Scotsman, had been detailed to a week's fatigue duty for some minor infraction of the rules. This meant a good deal of scrubbing and cleaning and slop-carrying. It also meant no exercise in the yard, for the adjutant had so arranged the fatigue party's routine that they were emptying the slop pails from the rooms of the other prisoners at this moment. So Stewart, although he lived in a different part of the prison, would now be in Lennox's room. That was a good plan. In the event of an escape the men who were examined most carefully were always those occupying the same quarters as the man who had escaped. Suspicion fell naturally on them.

"Thanks," Lennox said. "Thank you, Dusty." He stared at a small white cloud, already tinged red round its soft edges. The sun would soon go down. The bell would ring any minute now. "What did it cost you to get them?"

"Nothing," Miller answered. "Johann doesn't take bribes."

Lennox's eyebrows went up. "A jailer who doesn't take bribes?" he asked mockingly.

Miller's good-natured face was frowning. "He's all right, I tell you," he said shortly. After all, he thought, I've been working in the post office for months now. I've seen Johann every day. I ought to know what he's like. "If it hadn't been for him and his information we'd never have known about the capture of Sicily or any of the recent news," he said. Then his frown cleared as he saw Lennox's eyes. Men got that way just before an attempt to escape: after they had perfected the main plan they would worry about the details unnecessarily. Miller pulled his sweater more closely round his neck. The first evening breeze from the mountains was shrewd. "Going to be damned cold here this winter," he said, looking down at his thin shorts. Like most of the men, he was still wearing the lightweight clothes in which he had fought in Africa. Warmer clothing had been promised, but then the commandant always promised. And now it was the beginning of September, and the cold autumn rains would soon lash the unheated prison. "If we are still here," he added, and half smiled as he glanced at Lennox's face for a moment. "Something's blowing up, judging from the calm all round us today. Reminds me of

the Sunday when Musso resigned. Something's blowing
up."

Lennox didn't seem to think the idea was so very
funny. "Yes," he said grimly. "Maybe peace will be
signed and you'll all ride out of here while I'm still
squirming through ditches."

"Oh, we'll stop and give you a lift in our borrowed
Bugatti," Miller said generously. He was grinning openly
now as he watched the game of football. He laughed
more than necessary when the sergeant major missed
another shot at goal. Then, suddenly, he was serious
again.

"Don't worry, Pete. You'll make it. Good luck to you,"
he said as he rose. "This will be the last time I'll get a
word with you, I suppose."

Peter Lennox said "Yes." It was the habit of those
who were about to make an escape to avoid in the last
few days the friends who had helped them. It averted
suspicions and shortened the punishments for the men
left behind. "Thanks, Dusty."

For a moment the two friends looked at each other.
Then the New Zealander moved away as slowly, as
desultorily as he had come. He was talking to Ferry, the
South African, now: they were still chatting when the
bell began its mournful peal. The sentries, usually nagging the men to march quickly inside, were less urgent
today. Lennox picked himself up slowly and joined the
tail end of the straggling crowd. He had his last look at
the Dolomite ranges. Well, he thought, it wouldn't be
long before he might look at them as a free man. With
luck and care, it wouldn't be long.

Then he noticed that the two sentries outside the wire
were no longer bored. They were staring at the road,
some hundred yards across the grass from the outer wire.
Lennox and the men beside him stared too. Three large
army trucks were coming swiftly towards the camp from

the direction of the town. And they were not Italian. They were German.

"Perhaps some boxes," a man beside Lennox suggested hopefully. "About time some more packages were arriving."

"The Germans don't act as the Italians' postmen," another said acidly. He muttered something under his breath about bloody optimists.

But speculation was silenced as Falcone, the least likeable of all the prison guards, appeared at the wide arch of doorway. He was a small, thin-faced man with a thick skin, which the Abyssinian campaign had stained into a permanent walnut color. Camp gossip said he suffered from flat feet, an unfaithful wife, stomach ulcers, and strong Fascist convictions. Today he seemed to be feeling the effect of all four ailments simultaneously. There was more than the usual violence in his voice. His mounting rage contrasted strangely with the lassitude of the five other guards.

The prisoners had to content themselves with an exchange of side glances, as they marched in obedience to Falcone's shouts through the stone cavern of a hall into the room where thin meals were doled out. Yet this was not the time for food. Usually at this hour of the afternoon those whose names had appeared on the day's letter list would be taken to the post office in the Administrative side of the building; those who were less fortunate would be marched to their rooms and locked into bare boredom to await their shift for the mess hall. And now they had been gathered together, jammed up against the long tables and fixed benches in a room which had never been built to contain so many at once. This break with routine stirred the men for a moment, but the sudden undercurrent of excitement ebbed away as the solid door, which separated this room from the hall, was closed decisively. There was coughing, shuffling of feet as men tried to keep their balance in the crowd. There was Falcone's vigilant eyes and sharp tongue calling "Attention!"

From the courtyard at the back of the castle came the sound of grinding brakes. The trucks had arrived. But speculation was already dying. The boarded windows blotted out sight of a sky stretching to freedom. Under the naked bulbs, with their wavering electric light, the prisoners' faces were still more haggard. The animation of the exercise yard had gone, and with it the moment's forgetfulness. Here they remembered again.

CHAPTER 2

The men waited, outwardly patient (so much they had learned during their captivity) even if their thoughts were unprintable, and chalked up another petty annoyance on the Italian score. There weren't any cases of open brutality at this camp. Not since the Swiss representative had two of the worst bullies removed from the guardroom. The rest of the jailers weren't so bad, considering how bad the deposed two had been; for the most part they were inoffensive creatures, with weak hearts and stout stomachs, determined to keep their jobs so pleasantly far from the battlefield, and not averse to stretching their own rations with a pilfered package or two. The prisoners had been quick to learn; a package with a tin of meat or a slab of chocolate neatly filched out while it was being examined for contraband, meant a bribable jailer. Not that judicious bribing meant real kindness. But it did mean a cigarette from the town, or some little item which the camp commissary didn't have on sale, even if the price charged by the obliging jailer secured him a 600 per cent profit.

The minutes passed. The men were still held to attention. Then the uneasy silence was broken suddenly, and the men's thoughts switched from their own grievances over to the dulled sound of heavy boots shuffling through the hall outside. Peter Lennox's eyes left Falcone's savage little face and turned towards the door. Its solid thickness depressed him still more. What's going on? he wondered again. Whatever it was, he didn't like it. Any new developments in this camp meant complications in his escape. It was too near, he thought, it was too near. . . . The nagging worry of today and yesterday suddenly sharpened into anger.

"Hell!" Ferry said suddenly, and relaxed ostentatiously. That would mean another two weeks of "solitary" in a basement cell. Ferry had only recently completed such a turn. But his name had been on the letter list this morning, and he hadn't received any mail for over four months. "Hell!" he said again, and stared into Falcone's bulging eyes.

"And hell!" another voice said. Someone laughed, and the laughter increased. The Italian guards glanced uneasily at each other: here was another of these mad outbursts by the *Inglesi*. It began with nothing; just a laugh like this one now. And then it would spread into a chant—no violence, just chanting. You hadn't any justification for shooting at them. The most you could do, if you didn't want the Swiss to complain about the way this camp was run, was to choose the ringleaders (the basement cells being unfortunately inadequate in number for all the prisoners) and shut them up in darkness for a week or two. You could also cancel all privileges for the rest of the camp, and keep them confined to quarters. That was the most you could do: but the prisoners either couldn't or wouldn't learn.

Of all the guards Falcone enjoyed these outbursts least. He always seemed to think that they were an insult specially directed against his dignity. Now his dark face turned into a ripe pomegranate. The veins in his neck swelled. His hand was on his revolver. As the chorus of "Where are our letters? Where are our letters?" increased in volume his voice rose and was all the more ludicrous lost in the uproar. His eyes turned towards the doorway. He was worried as well as angry, almost nervous. Those who noticed that look paused for a moment, and then resumed their song with still greater enthusiasm. I'm a fool, Lennox was thinking: we'll be jugged for this, and the chances to escape will be more difficult. I'm a fool. . . . But the intoxication of this moment of small triumph, of seeing Falcone no longer assured and somehow shaken, couldn't be resisted. His voice joined the chorus even as he told himself just what size of a fool he was.

As the door half opened the men realized at last what had been worrying Falcone. The commandant himself had come, fat of face, sad-eyed, with his pouting lips ready to say so very gently "Such bad boys!" That was his usual phrase when he was about to order the meanest form of punishment he could give. But somehow, today the words weren't spoken. Lennox thought, he's worried too— What is wrong, anyway? The Italians hadn't lost so much composure since the day that Mussolini's fall was announced over the Rome radio, and the prisoners had all started a song with scurrilous additions about Humpty Dumpty. (It was after this unfortunately frank radio announcement that the wireless set in the prisoners' dining room suddenly went out of order and was never repaired. Since then the only news had come through Johann's asides to Miller, working beside him in the post office.) What was wrong, anyway? The other men near Lennox had sensed something too. They might still be prisoners, and these Italians were their keepers, but in this minute it was the prisoners who were victorious. Their answer was given once more by the door. It opened fully, and the prisoners could see a line of uniformed men, slowly filing through the hall towards the staircase. There were some heavily armed guards. There was an officer, now standing in the doorway. He was German. So were the strange guards. But the men in the dining room staring into the hall at the slowly moving file there stopped their chanting.

"British," Miller was yelling. "Canadian."

"American," Ferry added to that. "Hi there, Yanks!"

"And officers," Lennox heard his own voice shouting. The men stared, each at his neighbor. "Officers? What's the bright idea?" "Officers? what are they doing here?"

The German captain looked savagely at the Italian commandant. "What discipline!" he said. "Keep those men quiet." He turned to Falcone. "Keep these men quiet. What's wrong?"

"They want their letters—"

"Give them their letters." And then the captain turned to the prisoners, now silenced by their curiosity. "Any more of this and we will consider it mutiny. We will shoot." To the Italian guards he said, "Keep your guns ready."

"But—" the commandant began.

"No time for 'buts.' Give them their letters. Send that man for them." He pointed to Falcone. "At once!"

Falcone, taking the short cut to the post office, moved quickly through the back door of the mess hall into the kitchen.

The German captain looked around the room, his eyes narrowed. He spoke once more to the commandant. "Keep them quiet." His tone was so savage that Lennox, Miller, Ferry, and a score of others exchanged glances. The rest of the prisoners were either content that they were to be given the letters, or were still speculating why any officers should be brought to this camp. But Ferry and Miller had a different look in their eyes, and there was a grin on their lips. They were guessing, and the guesses were very comforting.

"Shut up," Lennox said quietly to the clown next him, who could only think of raising a smile at this moment by his "Officers? What next? I'm going to complain to the management."

"Shut up." And then as the man looked at him with a blank expression, he said quickly, "They can't have enough guards. They've got to bribe us to keep quiet.

They can't even detail guards to take us to the post office. So shut up. And get ready. Pass the word along."

The man still stared, but he obeyed, talking in the prison way, as Lennox had done, with his lips scarcely moving.

The German officer sensed a stirring in the mass of men in front of him, but their faces seemed quite expressionless. A rabble of common soldiers, he was thinking, and thank God for that; they would take orders, they knew nothing. He turned back to the entrance hall, leaving the commandant to hover hesitatingly in the doorway.

Lennox heard the German suddenly curse. "What's this now?" he was demanding of one of his own men. The commandant's curiosity moved his bulk through the doorway into the hall. Once more the prisoners who stood near the door could see the beginning of the staircase. The file of Allied officers was no longer ascending. The new arrivals were sitting on the steps, holding their bundles of possessions on their knees. They looked as if they were enjoying themselves immensely. Their innocence was too bland to be natural.

As the German captain stood hesitating, his eyes narrowed, his hands on his hips, a lazy American voice said to him mockingly, "Sorry, General, but there's a traffic jam."

One of the Englishmen said, "The rooms have not been cleared upstairs. We may as well sit down. We have a long journey ahead of us into Germany." He had raised his voice for the last sentence, and it carried clearly into the dining room. He smiled as he saw from the expression on the faces of the prisoners, who stood nearest to the door, that they had heard his words. And they had understood his meaning. These British and American officers were being shipped into Germany from Italy. Their appearance here was an emergency halt on that journey. They had been unexpected, and their arrival had thrown the camp into an uproar.

There was a burst of angry German commands. And then, in answer to them, a Scots voice shouted clearly downstairs, "We're doing the best we can. Tell your own ten chaps to do it if you're no' pleased." Now that look of quiet enjoyment on the officers' faces was explained, too. This delay in the clearing of some rooms for them was no accident. Jock Stewart and his fatigue party had been detailed by the Italians to throw the soldiers' possessions out, so as to make room for the new arrivals. And the officers had passed word upstairs to tell Stewart and his party to take as long as possible. And unless the Germans (*ten,* Stewart had obligingly reported) actually did the work themselves, Stewart would see to it that it would take as long as possible.

It was then that the commandant collected enough of his wits to close the door. The noises from the hall became muffled once more. All that could be heard was the shouting of the German guards, now subdued by the thick door into a blur of sound.

Ten of them, Lennox repeated to himself. Stewart had thought it important enough to say the exact number. There were five Italian guards in here; and there should be thirty-five other Italian guards around the camp, not to count the civilians who were employed either in the post office or in the commissary or in the kitchen. Yet, come to think of it, there hadn't been many Italians on view this afternoon. And when Falcone had left this room he had gone through the kitchen. And the kitchen was empty. Usually you could hear the Italians in there a mile off, as they wrangled over the share of the prisoners' supplies before they started cooking. But this afternoon there was only silence. This afternoon there had been fewer guards round the wire fences. No movements had come from the watchtower overlooking the walls. No movement from the guardroom.

Lennox felt his throat close in his excitement. His

humorous neighbor was being serious for once. "What's it all about?" he was asking.

Lennox stared at the heavy door which shut this room off from the hall. Behind there lay the answer. The officers knew; and Stewart and his party must have learned from them, for they knew. Here, one could only guess. But the door blocked contact. If the men in here and the men outside could act simultaneously there would be a chance to escape. Not for one, but for all of them.

"A chance," Lennox was saying, "a chance." He was now staring at the Italians' guns. Had Ferry guessed? Had Miller? If so there was indeed a chance. The humorist was looking at him. "What chance?" he kept repeating.

The kitchen door opened. But it wasn't Falcone who entered. It was the boy Johann, a small bundle of letters in his hand, a bright smile on his round face, now flushed with excitement. He was alone. He moved quickly towards the middle of the wall along which the guards stood, their guns held ready as the captain had commanded, and then turned to face the men. He spoke as quickly as he had moved, and, strangely enough, he spoke in the Italian which he had been forced to learn at school. Lennox suddenly realized that Johann was talking more for the benefit of the Italians than for the roomful of men, only a tenth of whom could understand his words.

"I brought the letters, for there was no one else to bring them." Johann's smile broadened, as he watched the Italians' faces. Miller was saying, "What's up? Johann, what's up?" Ferry was shouting, "Where's Falcone, where are the other guards?"

Johann was still watching the Italians. He said, "All are gone. One after another. Just slipping away. Like that." He moved his hand slowly in an arc, as if tracing the course of a sun which had risen, had stood high, and was now falling out of sight.

One of the Italians, with less will to believe than the others, said, "You lie." But his voice didn't sound too sure.

"Me?" Johann handed the small bundle of letters over to Miller, who didn't even begin to distribute them. The others had forgotten about the letters too. They were as silent as the Italians, but there was hope and expectancy in the prisoners' faces.

"Why," Johann was saying casually, "if you had been listening to the radio during the last half-hour, you would have heard the German announcement. It said just what I said when I came back from Bolzano this afternoon. Only some of you would believe me then. Now all, except you five dolts, believe me."

"We have capitulated?" one guard asked slowly.

"Unconditionally," Johann answered, with high good humor. "Unconditionally." He was obviously fond of that word.

There was the beginning of a shout from the prisoners. Those who hadn't understood the language fully had yet understood the meaning. There was little need for those who were translating so enthusiastically.

Johann pointed warningly towards the hall. *"Warten Sie noch!"* he said in his own language. Miller and Ferry silenced the impatient men. "Not yet, not yet!" Miller repeated.

Peter Lennox watched Johann uneasily. Was he with them, or against them? "Wait," he had said. But why wait? This chance might slip away. Now was the time. Why wait? Had this boy some plan which he had brought back from Bozen as well as the first news of the surrender? Or was he only enjoying this moment as any Tyrolese against the hated Italians?

One of the guards had tightened his grip on his gun. A hard, clever look came over his face as he kept the rifle pointed at the mass of men. He backed slowly towards the hall door. Three others wavered, and then followed his example. Peter Lennox cursed silently. The chance was slipping. The guards should have been rushed when the first shock of the news was upon them. Only, the prisoners had been too surprised themselves to be able to act then. Now there was only silence in the room.

"Fools!" Johann said quietly, looking at the hall door. "No help for you there. The Germans are calling the Italians traitors. They are killing Italians in Naples."

The guard, who had almost reached the hall door, paused.

"The Germans are killing Italians, and the Italians are killing Germans," Johann said very slowly. He was enjoying the idea so much that the Italians knew he spoke the truth. "Look," he went on, now urgent and serious, "I give you warning, more warning than you gave my friends when you seized them for your army in Albania and in Greece. I give you fair warning. The Germans are taking over Northern Italy. The Italians are leaving Bolzano. The South Tyrol is no longer Italian."

The guards were staring now at the boy's triumphant smile. For over twenty years the Italians had tried to make the South Tyrol a part of Italy. Now, if their authority were removed, the Tyrolese would have a long-remembered score to settle. So the guards were silent, as if numbed by the fear which must have tormented them for many weeks now. The fear had been too real, too well-earned, to let them have any doubts of the truth in Johann's words. First one, and then the others left the hall door, and backed slowly along the wall towards the kitchen entrance. Their guns were no longer truculent. They were no longer the jailers. These prisoners didn't matter now that the war was over. There was only one purpose now, and that was to reach the Italy where Italians lived. The guards, admitting that, measured their own imminent danger. It grew with each hour of delay.

Lennox watched the strangely silent men, whose slow,

uncertain movements were now beginning to take the shape of hurry.

As they reached the kitchen door Johann spoke softly. "Your guns will show you are deserters. Best leave them here, so that if you meet any Germans they will think you are only going off duty."

The Italians hesitated.

"All right. Don't believe me," Johann said. "Find out for yourselves. The only Italians who keep their guns are those who are going to fight the Germans. The Germans know that. But find it out for yourselves." He held out his hand for the weapons. The Yorkshire sergeant major, pushing his way through the mass of prisoners, pulled a rifle out of an unresisting hand and pointed with his thumb to the kitchen door.

"Go on," he said encouragingly. "We won't shoot you." The Italians hadn't understood his words, but they caught their meaning. They went, with a haste so precipitous that even the sergeant major looked somewhat amazed at the five rifles stacked in his arms.

Lennox felt an emotion which was almost pity. It isn't pleasant to see men realize that they are trapped and helpless, that now it's their turn to be kicked about. And then he was telling himself to keep his pity for those who deserved it. None of these guards had ever done a spontaneous, decent thing for any of the prisoners: their occasional kindnesses had been granted when the payment—in food from the prisoners' boxes—had been exorbitantly extracted. Humanity had been lowered to the level of barter and grab. Even now none of the guards had volunteered to fight along with the prisoners: now they were only thinking of how to save their own skins and property as they scrabbled their way through the kitchen door. Let him keep his pity for those who had practised pity.

There was a movement as if the prisoners had decided something too. The mass of men came to life. Even those who were ill, who had propped their bodies against the tables in the room, watched with eager eyes. They were waiting, ready.

Miller, talking urgently to Johann, had now started to tell the sergeant major the boy's suggestion. It had sufficient possibilities, because the sergeant major nodded and selected five men. Johann, it seemed, was to be entrusted with a gun; he and the five men were already leaving the room by the kitchen door. Lennox edged his way to where Miller stood.

"What's the idea?" he asked, more quietly than he felt. Fool, he was thinking, to sacrifice a gun to Johann. . . . What good would that do?

"They will reach the courtyard through one of the kitchen doors. There are three German lorries under guard in the courtyard."

It wasn't a very perfect explanation. Miller was too busy trying to persuade the sergeant major that he could use a rifle as well as the next man. But the word "courtyard" caught Lennox's ear. In the courtyard was the guardhouse, where other weapons, including machine guns, could be found. The five men would march in good order across the courtyard, as if they had been detailed for some camp duty. If the Germans guarding their lorries were to turn their attention on the prisoners, then Johann, armed and in correct uniform, would give the authentic touch of control to the scene. The Germans were strangers here and ignorant of the camp's routine.

"What about the Italians in the guardroom?"

"Gone. So Johann said."

Lennox's mouth twisted. "So Johann said," he mimicked, but Miller had followed the others, who, realizing that the remaining guns could only arm four men, were now invading the deserted kitchen. Quickly they passed out to the mess hall any choppers, pans, ladles, rolling pins, they could find. Ferry was testing a carving knife thoughtfully; Miller had compromised on a meat mallet. Lennox refused a Chianti bottle and made his way into the kitchen to choose his own weapon. He came back into the dining room gripping in his left hand a length of iron chain which had once held a soup pot suspended over the kitchen fire. He knotted it loosely at the end, and a slow grin came over his tight mouth as he tested the chain's weight. He glanced at his taut wrist. His watch said it was now thirty-five minutes past six. Johann had brought the letters at six-twenty-six. Nine minutes had passed. Nine minutes against seven months. Seven months of worry and sweat to prepare for an escape. And here it was in nine minutes, flat.

The sergeant major held up his hand. He was standing at the hall door, ready to swing it open.

To the three sharpshooters he had chosen he said, "I take the captain. You, the man to his left. You, the man to his right. You, the German at the top of the stairs. After that, pick off the nearest. You others, start rushing when we stop shooting. When I give the signal everyone yell his bloody head off. Ready, boys?"

The men nodded, and tightened their grasp round their weapons. Those who had nothing but their bare hands gathered together in a solid mass behind the crudely armed spearhead.

The sergeant major held his hand raised. He's waiting, Lennox guessed, for the courtyard; the men who had marched towards the guardroom with Johann should have taken possession of the machine guns by this time. He glanced quickly at the tense, waiting faces around him, and then at his watch. Another minute and a half had gone. His muscles tautened, and he felt a drop of perspiration trickle over his upper lip. He stared at the door as the others did. Each slipping second could spell disaster.

From the courtyard there came the sharp, uneven rattle of a machine gun. The diversion had begun.

The sergeant major's arm dropped. Someone knocked the door's latch free, someone swung the heavy mass of oak wide open. The four sharpshooters were already taking aim as they entered the hall. The men surged forward. They were shouting. The haggard faces were alive once more.

CHAPTER 3

In the hall the German captain had placed six of his men in a well-spaced line to flank the curve of stairway. Their guns were pointed towards the row of officers, still waiting patiently, expectantly. Two other German soldiers guarded the head of the staircase. Their guns pointed too, but their eyes kept glancing sideways along the upstairs corridor, in which the angry voices of the two remaining Germans were combined with the sounds of a rough-and-ready removal.

The captain, standing at the foot of the staircase, was obviously angry. His fury increased as his patience evaporated. He fingered his revolver. Another minute of this impudence and he would order his men upstairs to shoot. If only these damned Anglo-Saxons would make one move then his men's guns would have an answer for them. But they gave no appearance of mutiny, no excuse for shooting. They just sat and stared at him calmly. Impudence—that was it. Some of them were even smiling: that American up there was grinning broadly. Damn these Italians and their lax discipline. If only they had had their full quota of guards when his party had arrived here the rooms upstairs would have been ready by this time. And if only the damned Americans hadn't bombed the Brenner railway line yesterday the damned train carrying the prisoners wouldn't now be held up at Bozen until the damned line could be repaired. He glared at the Italian commandant. He'd tell this fat bucking jackass a thing or two, once they had the prisoners all safely locked up.

The commandant fingered the decorations on his tunic and cleared his throat. But the German's angry face silenced the beginning of an apology. The commandant even stopped fingering his decorations. This captain hadn't even treated him as an officer of superior rank. The smothered apology turned sour in his mouth. With stilted dignity he walked over to the wall, and looked at the mass of foreigners with distaste. Two years ago everything had been so different. The tears filming his eyes as he thought of that change dried in alarm. He had suddenly remembered that he still had to explain to this German that the Italian guards, now away from the camp, were absent without leave. Deserters . . . he hadn't dared mention that word. He sighed wearily. He wished he were upstairs in his pleasant room, listening to his wireless set: he might have learned by this time if this afternoon's rumors were true or false. Then he would know what to do. He glared at the smiling Allied officers. His heart suddenly twisted as he thought of his country at the mercy of barbarians. His eyelids drooped. He held his weakening underlip rigid with his teeth. He studied the floor at his feet, as if he could read there why his Italy should suffer such unhappiness, such injustice.

There was the sudden rattle of a machine gun in the courtyard.

All heads turned sharply to the entrance door of the hall.

"Watch the prisoners!" the German captain shouted. "You there—anyone who moves will be shot. Meyer, Hofmann, with me!" He started smartly towards the courtyard. Probably only an Italian trying to desert, he thought, and his pace hesitated. The commandant's eyes lifted and met his, and the German saw the same thought in them. There was fear, too, and shame.

Perhaps there was more than one deserter, the German thought, perhaps that was why this fat fool had acted so strangely ever since the unexpected arrival of prisoners in this camp. Perhaps there was a lot of trouble here to be settled. He was staring with increasing suspicion at the Italian, and so he did not see the broad thick door of the mess hall as it opened. But he saw the Italian's eyes dilate. He heard the beginning of a shout, and turned, and fell. The Yorkshire sergeant major had aimed well.

The commandant stared at the German captain's body, lying so still and now forever humbled. The two soldiers who had followed the captain had crumpled on to the paved floor. Blood trickled slowly. The commandant stared incredulously. Other shots crashed through the hall, deafening, terrifying. He was scarcely aware that the staircase was a seething mass of officers, that the hall was filled with sweating, cursing, ragged men. He stared at two bodies falling from above, as if two sacks of flour had been thrown over the balustrade, and then remembered the two Germans who had guarded the head of the staircase. He could not hear the hard thud of their bodies on the stone floor so near his feet: the volume of noise in the hall was smashing into his ears, puckering his face with fear and pain. These yelling savages swarming towards him . . . these answering yells from upstairs, telling that the last Germans had been dealt with. . . .

Then, suddenly, out of the mass of noise and movement, he saw one of his prisoners run towards him. He felt naked in his helplessness, alone with savages. Savages. His muscles obeyed him at last. He ran from the prisoner, from the swinging piece of chain. He ran towards the entrance. Out there in the courtyard the Germans would help him. They'd machine-gun these savages. They would cut them down like ripe hay.

The door opened as he reached it, and he saw men advancing towards him out of the courtyard. The light from the hall gleamed on a machine gun. A sob of relief rose from his tight throat. And then he recognized them. . . . They were *Inglesi*.

Another figure came running out of the darkness.

"Schichtl!" the commandant shouted. But as he saw the boy's face his sudden hope died.

Johann raised his arm and fired his gun. The commandant's face was blotted out. He hadn't even had time to wonder why such injustice should be happening to him.

Johann stepped over the commandant's body. "Come on," he said to the three Britishers. "Come on." His tone was even and urgent.

One of the men gave a low whistle of admiration. "Make up your mind quick, don't you?"

"Come on."

But inside the hall there was no need to set up the machine gun. All resistance had ceased. The irrepressible man gave another whistle. "Like Christmas night in the workhouse," he said cheerily.

No one else spoke. Some men were picking themselves up from the floor. Five—including the sergeant major— were wounded badly. Two were as motionless as the Germans. The rest just stood, and stared. After the uproar of the last two minutes the silence was like death itself. Then someone raised a cheer. It was a thin, pathetic effort. But the others joined in, and the cheer swelled almost to a shout. Then everyone was as suddenly silent again, looking sheepishly at one another, beginning to move round the hall. One of the American Air Force officers said, "We're a funny-looking bunch all right," and a laugh began. Men laughed for no reason at all.

But the American had spoken the truth. They were a strange collection. They had been civilians in countries as far distant from each other as they were from Italy. They had become soldiers. Craftsmen, workmen, businessmen, professional men, had learned how to march and shoot and drive a tank, how to handle artillery or a parachute or an airplane. They wore the faded, stained

uniforms of the veteran. Their bodies were thin, their
faces were gaunt. But the look of the prisoner—the
desperate, self-tortured look of the forgotten man—had
vanished. They were laughing for no reason at all, but
they laughed like free men.

Peter Lennox didn't laugh. He was kneeling beside
Miller when Johann came up to him.

The boy's excited face became grave too. He bent
down and touched Miller's brow. He drew back his hand
quickly, and his mouth became set. He said nothing. He
straightened his back and stood quietly there, looking
down at the dead man's face. There was a band of white
flesh at the edge of Miller's hair, where even the desert
sun hadn't managed to reach the skin. You saw it clearly
now, as he lay with his head thrown stiffly backward. The
blue eyes stared up at the damp stone ceiling.

Lennox glanced at Johann Schichtl's broad-boned face,
impassive and yet somehow all the more expressive. The
boy kept his silence. Miller had been right, Lennox
thought. Miller had liked and trusted this boy. And this
boy had really liked Miller. Johann suddenly looked at
him, and Lennox felt ashamed of his initial distrust, of
his unreasoning dislike of the boy. He looked quickly
down again at Miller, and tried to straighten his friend's
body into a decent sleep.

"Who's this?" an officer was asking. His voice was
hard, his hand was on Johann's shoulder.

CHAPTER 4

"Who's this fellow?" the officer repeated. His faded insig-
nia showed he was a captain in the Tank Corps.

Lennox rose to his feet, and unconsciously stood beside Johann. Something in the officer's high-pitched voice,
in his way of repeating the question so insistently, annoyed Lennox. What did he think Lennox was? A blasted
idiot? Johann wouldn't have been alive if he had been an
enemy. Lennox remembered Miller's words that afternoon. He repeated them now. "He's all right," he said,
and then remembered to add "sir." Johann's anxious face
was turned towards him. The boy's light blue eyes were
worried as he listened to the English voices. The officer's
hand left his shoulder, and the worried look eased.

"He's a friend, sir," the captain reported in his turn to
a colonel who was watching the group curiously.

The colonel nodded. "Where are all the guards?" he
asked Lennox.

"They left before the fight started, sir," Lennox answered. He looked bitterly at the officers' insignia. All
that old stuff again, sirs and salutes and sirs. "Johann,
here, scared the daylight out of them with the news."

"And what was that?" the colonel asked quickly.

"The South Tyrol is no longer Italian."

The colonel half smiled and glanced at Johann's face.
"And Johann belongs to the South Tyrol?"

"Yes, sir."

"Any other news? We heard rumors of peace on our
journey north."

"The Eyties have surrendered, sir."

The officers exchanged broad grins. "Better tell the others," the senior officer said. "And tell them there's no more fighting to be done here meanwhile. Seemingly the rest of the guards have upped and left us." He stood watching Johann. "I'd like to see you once we straighten things out here," he said in very precise German.

Johann looked worried. He answered quickly, and at some length.

"What the dickens is he talking about?" the colonel asked in amazement.

"I didn't catch all of it, sir, but I think he was saying that he wants to leave now. He says he has proved that we can trust him."

"Yes, but he's just the chap we need. Tell him to stay here meanwhile. Better keep him inside. You seem to understand his lingo."

"I've got accustomed to the accent, sir."

"Well, stay with him. We want to be sure we don't misunderstand him when we have time to question him."

Lennox said, "Yes, sir." He spoke without any enthusiasm. He had a uniform upstairs. He had a map and money. He had his plan. Now would be the time to use them. Darkness was coming, and he could have been far from here by daybreak. He would have managed it, too; this time he would have escaped. It was just his blasted luck, he thought; seven months of planning for nothing. And then, as he saw Miller lying at his feet, his lips tightened, and he stopped grousing about his luck.

The colonel had looked at Lennox keenly for a moment before he turned away to attend to the decisions which were being carried out. As senior officer, he had much to organize quickly.

The wounded were taken to be patched up in the camp hospital across the courtyard. The dead were carried out of the hall, and the Germans' weapons, uniforms, and papers were removed for future use. Extra men were sent out to join the two who had remained on guard over the captured lorries. A detail was dispatched to the kitchen and storerooms to forage for food. Officers were in the commandant's office, examining papers and maps. One of them was installed at the telephone: he had taught Romance languages at a university, and could cope with any sudden calls to the commandant from the town. Another, who had been an advertising artist, was making sketches of various sections of the enormous relief map which was cemented into one wall of the office. A party had gone down the blackness of the detention cells, where they found the jailer had long left his basement post, and seventeen cold, filthy, and truculent Tommies were helped upstairs. Others searched the castle and out-buildings with care. The guardroom was emptied of weapons and ammunition. The commissary was ransacked for useful equipment. Armed sentries, in German coats, were posted round the camp. The searchlight at the gate was manned, ready to give its usual five-minute sweep, so that any Germans in the town would see its customary watchfulness.

The men and officers accomplished their jobs quickly and efficiently. But there was an underlying cheerfulness which would break out into a laugh, or a quip, or an exchange of good-natured libels. The younger officers were as excited as the men. Only the senior officer, and the two majors who stood talking to him, were grave. Only Lennox and Johann Schichtl, standing together in the hall, were silent. And both were equally impatient.

But when the colonel came over to them once more he didn't waste much time in finding out what he wanted to know. Johann, in spite of his obvious impatience, answered each question quickly and directly. Lennox translated, when necessary, with equal simplicity. The officers, grouped round the colonel, watched the boy's face as they listened to Lennox.

First of all, they were assured, they need have no

fears about Falcone or the five guards who had been the last to desert from the camp, and who were the only Italians to see the revolt begin. For these men had been strong Fascists like the commandant. They would never reach the town. ("We've taken care of that," Johann said with a grin. "It is easier to kill them now than to have to search them out later.")

Those who had deserted earlier in the day had slipped away, one by one, each thinking he was the only man with foresight in the camp. And so each would believe that the camp was still guarded by those he had left behind.

None of the Germans in the courtyard had escaped to give warning.

No house was near the camp, and no one in the town could have heard the shots.

No one would come to the camp tonight. The first arrivals would be at six tomorrow morning, when the daily food supplies were brought to the camp.

The staffs of the kitchen, commissary, and post office, who were civilians recruited from the town, generally arrived at seven o'clock each morning.

So much for the camp's routine and personnel.

As to the town (*"Bozen,"* Johann said pointedly, as the colonel again made the tactical error of using the Italian form of Bolzano), only Italians had occupied the barracks until recently. After Mussolini's fall some Germans had been placed in command. That was what caused the trouble in the town this afternoon. The Italian soldiers had said the war was over. They had put down their guns and tried to walk out. The Germans had shot at them. And then the Italian officers, who until then were not sure what they should do, had ordered their men to shoot back. There were not many Germans in the barracks so they were all killed. A number of Italians were killed, too, and the rest had left the barracks. Some of them had taken rifles and ammunition, but many didn't.

These had stripped off their uniforms, and had left their guns in the barracks. They were pretending now to be civilians.

The Nazis would probably take over the town, for they were already in firm control of the station and the railway to the Brenner Pass. They were playing a double game: they were backing the Fascist Italians, who were still working with the Nazis, and they were trying to win the support of the Tyrolese. Some of the Tyrolese listened to the Germans, believing that Hitler would free them from the Italians as his secret propaganda had promised for many years. But other men of the Tyrol only saw the Germans as new dictators to oppress them.

When Johann ended the colonel exchanged glances with the two majors. "At least," he said, with a wry smile, "we are probably safe enough here for the next few hours. We have time to eat and finish our plans."

One of the majors—he was an American wearing Rangers' insignia—said, "But it's a hell of a setup."

The other major nodded. "Absolutely." He looked at Johann again. "It seems we have three kinds of Italians to deal with. Those who won't fight at all; those who won't fight against the Germans; and those who want to fight the Germans. And there are two kinds of Tyrolese: those who are pro-Nazi, mainly because they hate the Italians; and those who hate the Nazis and who want to get rid of the Italians by themselves. That gives us five different sets of people to handle, not to mention the Germans."

"Personally," the American said, "I'll be glad when we come up against the Germans. At least, you know what to shoot there."

The colonel was still watching Johann. Half to himself he said, "If we only knew more about politics here we might be able to—" He turned to Lennox. "Do you know anything about the political quarrels in this district?"

"A little. But Johann could tell you much more, sir."

"If we had time . . . " the colonel said. "If I were sure
of enough time . . . " He had started worrying again.
"Pass out the food, anyway," he said to the majors.
"Share round any weapons you've found. Make a division
of the men into those who are fit to travel and fight,
those who are not. Find out their special branch of the
service and decide how we can best use them."

The officers hurried away. The colonel still watched
Johann.

"Let me question him, sir," Lennox said suddenly,
and his suggestion surprised himself as much as the
colonel.

"Go ahead," the older man said. He watched Lennox
with thoughtful eyes.

Lennox said quietly, "Johann, who told you to give
the prisoners information? Who told you to spread the
news among the guards so that they'd desert? Someone
you met down in Bozen, when you were off duty today?"

A careful look spread over Johann's face, and wiped
all the emotion out of it.

"Someone told you, didn't he, Johann?"

Johann didn't answer. I bet I'm right, Lennox was
thinking. Johann was no fool; but there was a cleverer
man than he would ever be behind all this.

"I must leave," Johann was saying. "I must go now.
I have told you everything. I must go."

"To see this man?" tried Lennox.

Johann looked at him unhappily. "Our plans have
changed. I must report," he admitted.

"Changed? You mean the Germans who arrived here
and are now killed have altered the plans?"

Johann said nothing.

"But, Johann, they are dead. They won't inform. How
can they alter any plans?"

Johann still said nothing.

Lennox looked at the officer. "Sorry, sir. That's as far
as we get."

"You didn't do badly. At least you've discovered the boy is part of an organization. Pity he has suddenly shut up like this. Might have been helpful."

Jock Stewart appeared with a rough bandage round his head and a stack of thick sandwiches in his arm. "Best chuck we've had here yet," he said cheerfully, and handed out the slabs of bread with their generous slices of cheese. "Eyties' larder," he explained. "Soup is being heated now. Won't be long, sir." Then as Lennox took his allotted sandwiches, Stewart suddenly said, "Hey! I've got something for you. Didn't get time to hide them before the Jerries arrived. There in my pocket. No. The left one."

Lennox obeyed. He pulled out the German buttons which Miller had got for him. They gleamed in his soot-smeared palm.

"Not much good to you now," Stewart said, with his usual combination of the practical and the obvious.

Lennox's lips tightened as he looked at the buttons. And then he saw that both the colonel and Johann were staring at them too.

"When did you plan to leave?" the colonel was asking quietly, almost sympathetically.

"Tomorrow or the next day, sir. Before the moon grew too big." Lennox made an attempt to smile. Suddenly he handed the buttons to Johann. "Perhaps you'll find someone else who needs them."

"They were for you?"

"Yes."

"Not for Miller?"

"No."

"For you? You were planning to escape?"

"I was." Seven months of work, of planning, of worrying. Seven months of self-centered concentration. That's what these seven months had done to him. That's all they had produced.

Johann's face changed. "Then *you* are the one we want.
Please come. The man you were asking about wants to
see you. Let us go at once. We are late. Very late."

The colonel had understood part of these words. "He
wants to see you?" He looked at the puzzled Lennox.
"That means he wants to see the man who was determined enough to escape from this prison camp." He
paused for a moment. And then, with a mental jump
which seemed at first inconsequential, he said, "I believe
any man sent here had a record of escapes from other
camps. And the corporal told me that any who tried to
escape from here were shot if they were found. Is that so?"

"Shot while resisting arrest," Lennox said bitterly.
"Their bodies were sent back here to prove that to the
others."

"But escaped prisoners are unarmed: weapons are the
one thing that a guard can't be bribed to procure."

"They were unarmed, sir."

"I see." The colonel was silent. Then to Johann he
said very carefully, "Why does this man in Bolzano—
Bozen, I mean—want to see the prisoner who planned
to escape? For what reason?"

Johann was undecided, hesitating, worried. And then,
as if realizing the quickest way to end all this questioning
was to give direct answers once more, he said simply,
"We need him. To go with us into the mountains. We
need him. When your armies will be coming up to the
Brenner Pass we need someone who can"—he fumbled
for the right word—"connect us with you."

Lennox translated the boy's sentences quickly. "Liaison
officer is what he means, I think," he concluded.

The boy nodded eagerly as he heard "liaison." "That's
the word. We need liaison. We are working alone. We
need somone to connect us with you, to tell you that we
are patriots and to be trusted. To tell you what we have
done and why we have done it. Or else the Allies would
think when they came that we were only joining the

winning side, that we hadn't earned the right to be masters in our own land."

Lennox translated again.

"So that's it!" the colonel said. Then, "Suppose we agreed to this, and gave you a liaison officer, would the man in Bozen help us now? When we leave here we will fight our way south to join our troops coming north. But we need more guns—many more. And we need help for the wounded who can't travel with us. Can your people help them?"

Johann considered these problems. "Perhaps. I don't know. He could tell you."

"Who is he?"

"The man in Bozen." And that was all Johann would say.

CHAPTER 5

The colonel began eating his sandwich. In between bites
he was talking to Lennox. He seemed to have forgotten
Johann. By the time he had finished his ration of food
he had learned that Peter Lennox was an infantry man,
enlisted in the Territorials in August 1939, who had
seen service in North Africa, Greece, Crete, and then
in North Africa again. He had been wounded and captured in the fall of Tobruk. He had been held in two
other Italian prison camps. Because of attempted escapes
he had been transferred to this one.

The colonel was thoughtful for a minute. Then he
asked suddenly, "What were you in civilian life?"

Lennox hesitated, and then—steeling himself against
the usual smile which his answer to that question always
roused—he answered, "I used to paint."

But the colonel didn't smile. He looked at the shape
of Lennox's hands. He noted the mocking scar on the
right hand. "An artist?"

"Yes, sir."

"Know your way around, abroad?"

"Some places, sir."

"Know Austria?"

"Yes, but not this part of the Tyrol."

"You know the Northern Tyrol?"

"Yes, sir."

"Know it well? Where did you stay?"

Lennox repressed a smile, remembering how little his

travels had to cost. "I stuck to out-of-the-way places, sir."
Not Salzburg. Not Innsbruck. Not St. Anton. Not for me.

"Would you say that you would find the North and
South Tyrol similar?"

Lennox stared. Whatever the reason for these questions
he didn't at all like it.

"Yes, sir. At least, I've seen many a Johann Schichtl
in the North. I think the most obvious difference is in
the shapes of the mountains."

The colonel was still watching him carefully. He asked
unexpectedly, "Didn't you try for a commission when
you joined the army?"

"I prefer this way, sir."

The colonel smiled at that. He wasn't so very surprised. He had already decided that this young man with
the shock of brown hair, hard gray eyes, and unsmiling
mouth had his own ideas about what he wanted to do.
Probably he had chosen to be a private in the infantry
because he obviously thought you suffered most as a
private in the infantry. Well, if this man thought service
was measured by suffering he certainly had served well.
The colonel wondered for a moment if Lennox had been
a pacifist in the nineteen-thirties. Probably.

And then the American major returned. His information wasn't pleasant. There had been nine men in the
hospital; three of them couldn't walk. Of the other prisoners, twenty-three were weakened by malaria. Of the
five wounded in the hall tonight, only two could travel.
They, like the malaria cases, would have to be considered
passengers. They weren't fit for active combat.

The colonel's face was tight and grim once more. He
was looking at Johann Schichtl, as if his eyes could gauge
the Austrian's worth. When time was short you had to
depend on your capacity to judge character by what you
saw in a man's face. The difficulty with Johann was that
he was still a boy, without any definite character written
on his round red-cheeked face. His blue eyes were honest

and eager. His mouth was capable of two expressions: a friendly curve and a rebellious line. At the moment it was the rebellious line which straightened his lips and gave his good-natured chin an angry, disappointed set.

The colonel turned to Lennox, and spoke in halting French. "You knew him for some months. Did you feel you could trust him?"

"I didn't trust him then, sir."

"But you trusted him this afternoon."

"Only since Miller was killed, sir."

The colonel stared. "You don't seem very clear about it," he said sharply in English.

"Yes, sir," Lennox agreed. The trouble is, he was thinking, when you tell people the truth they won't believe you. If he had said he trusted Johann because he had helped them against a batch of lousy Fascists he would have lied. He hadn't trusted Johann then. This afternoon Johann's politics had run a parallel course with the prisoners' hopes. That was why he had fought with them. You couldn't trust a man whose only thought was politics: he was only your friend as long as it suited him. But there had been something in the way Johann had stood and looked at the dead Miller, something of real feeling and sadness which had jolted Lennox out of his cynicism. There was decent good will in this boy. He could be trusted.

The colonel looked gloomily at his watch. "The time is now almost eight-fifteen. By the boy's information, we still have some hours of safety here. We shall have to trust him—that's all. We need friends. We shan't find them by refusing to meet them halfway."

He turned to the American. "You and Major Cummins take charge. I'm going into this Bolzano, or Bozen, or whatever it's called. I'll see this man and get his help. If I don't return by ten o'clock leave here. Don't wait one minute after ten."

The American major was looking worried now, in his turn.

"The wounded?" he asked.

"If I get back here there will be a plan for the wounded. This man in Bozen will have to take care of them. That's the price I'm going to ask for the man who is going up into the mountains as liaison officer."

"Why not send someone else in your place to Bozen?" the American suggested.

"Because I've got to make the decision about leaving a man with these Tyrolese. It's my responsibility. Besides I want to know just what we might expect when our armies reach this part of the country." The colonel smiled faintly as he added, "I am not at all so necessary for leading a party to the south. You and Cummins can do that as well as I could. And if I go myself to this man in Bozen then we are showing we are in earnest. We'll get quickest results that way."

He turned to Johann and asked, "How soon can we reach this man?"

Johann's smile came slowly back. "Twenty minutes on foot. Five minutes with the lorry," he said happily. "It will be safe enough if we wear German coats. Perhaps there will be something you could bring back in the lorry."

The officers looked at each other. "What could we bring back?" the colonel asked.

"The barracks in Bozen had much equipment." Johann was grinning cheerfully, and the officers were smiling too; their guess had been right. The answer was guns.

"Come along," the colonel said to Lennox. "I shall need you. And I'll need a couple of other fellows. Pick out two of the toughest men here. Two who understand some German."

Lennox obeyed without any enthusiasm. Hell, he was thinking, nothing ever goes the way you plan it. He would be stuck here for the rest of the war. He could see it

coming. If the colonel had his way—and who was to
stop a blasted colonel?—he would be left here in those
mountains while the others marched south. If only he
had been stupid, talked foolishly, pretended to know
nothing about Johann or his language. Too late now; he
had been a bright little boy, and his seven months of
planning had landed him among mountains.

"I'd like to—" began the American.

"Sorry, old man. You're needed here." The colonel
signed to two junior officers. "Cover that up with these,"
he ordered, pointing first to their commando uniforms
and then to the pile of German coats. He was no longer
worried. Now that the decision had been made he looked
even happy, as if he were going to enjoy himself. Blast
him, Lennox thought bitterly, and picked up a German
coat and cap as the two lieutenants had done.

The two men he chose were Ferry and Merriman.
(Stewart had to be passed over: his bandaged head would
have been too conspicuous.) They were as excited as
the lieutenants, and they had already covered their
bleached uniforms with the German coats. They were
smiling all over their faces as they left the hall. Johann,
as happy as anyone, waited at the door. The colonel,
strangely formidable in the German captain's long military coat, turned at last from the two majors and walked
towards Johann.

"Come on, there," he said quickly, over his shoulder.
"Step lively."

"Yes, sir," Lennox said. He looked at Stewart, who
was watching the departing men glumly. "You know
where I've hidden my coat, Jock. There's a good map,
and some money and other things behind the loose
board—the one that's covered by that calendar I made.
Perhaps you can use them."

Stewart gave him a sharp look. "I'll find a use for
them," he said. He clapped Lennox on the shoulder as

if he realized this was the last time they would see each other. "It's a damned shame," Stewart said. "It's . . ."

"Step lively!" the colonel yelled from the doorway.

Lennox nodded to Stewart, and then he was hurrying between the groups of men in the hall. He followed the colonel out into the night. Seven months, he was thinking bitterly. As he passed two German-like sentinels in the courtyard, and heard them wish him luck, he was wondering whether he would have managed to escape this time, or whether he would have made just another "shot-while-resisting" corpse. Third try was usually luck, it was said. But now he'd never know. He felt cheated. This thought was so busy rankling in his mind that he blundered in the darkness as he climbed onto the lorry, and the high mudguard struck sharply against his shin. He swore much more than was necessary, but at least he felt better. The colonel's taut wrist pulled him safely on board, down onto a hard wooden bench, as the lorry started impatiently forward. It swung through the gateway, past the watchtowers with their machine guns and the swinging searchlights, past the masses of ten-foot-high barbed wire. It jolted over the wooden bridge which spanned the deep, moatlike pit encircling the walls of wire.

"Do you smell that?" Ferry said in great awe.

"A tannery, I rather think," one of the lieutenants said.

"Maybe," Ferry said, and his voice was strained. He drew a long breath, as if to steady himself. "But it's free air to me."

The rest were silent. They huddled together as the lorry swung down the mountainside. The only sounds came from the wheels grinding over the loose stones on the surface of the road. The engine had been switched off. The lorry was running silently, depending on its brakes and Johann's skillful driving, down towards the town.

CHAPTER 6

Johann snapped his fingers to attract attention, and then pointed. The men's eyes followed the quick movement of the boy's outstretched arm, black against the dark-blue sky. The lorry was coming well down into the valley now. The road had twisted in long, serpentine loops as it descended through the vineyards. Houses had been few, and silent. All around were the dark silhouettes of heightening mountain peaks. Below them was the River Eisak, which the Italians had named Isarco, with its flat, narrow valley broadening as it reached the scattered lights of a town.

"Bolzano," the colonel said.

"Bozen," Johann insisted. Over his shoulder he said, "We shall halt the lorry soon, northeast of the town. The English officer and Lennox will come with me to see the man. That will only take ten minutes. The lorry will wait for us until we have seen him."

"And the barracks?" asked the colonel. Quick work, Lennox thought approvingly: the colonel was picking up Johann's way of speaking. He didn't need a translator now to help with the South Tyrol dialect twist in the words. Then why, Lennox demanded of the dark sky, why did he bring me down here? To reassure Johann? Or had Stewart's premonition been right? Lennox kept his gloomy silence, and listened to Johann's polite but adamant refusal to go near the barracks.

The lorry should be left on a side road on the outskirts of the town. It was just there that this man from Bozen

52

was waiting for Johann. And the man would be able to tell them whether it was safe to try to reach the barracks. (For the barracks, seemingly, lay on the south side of the town at the river's edge. To reach it, they would have either to pass the station, which certainly had been in German control this afternoon, or to make a detour through the center of the town.) Perhaps, Johann suggested with a smile, the barracks had even already been emptied of its arms and ammunition. The man at Bozen would know.

The colonel said nothing. But when Johann stopped in the shadow of some trees just where a rough track, emerging darkly from a small wood, joined the road they had followed, Lennox could almost feel the colonel's unwillingness to leave the lorry guarded by the four other men. His plan, like most bright ideas, seemingly excellent at the moment of discovery, was beginning to tarnish with each minute of delay. The colonel had started worrying again. The barracks were his chief objective: he disliked having them made into secondary importance.

"If anyone starts asking questions just remember to keep talking German," he said to the men. "Your story is that the lorry has broken down on your way back to the station after delivering the officers to the prison camp. Don't shoot, unless you are desperate. Get rid of any curious stranger quietly." The colonel looked round him. The countryside was peaceful, the isolated houses were dark and seemingly asleep even at this early hour. The lights in Bozen itself were scattered and dim: there were no shots, no shouts, to break through the deep silence of the night. The lorry was swallowed up in the trees' shadows. Anyone passing along the road wouldn't even notice it. All was well, so far. And yet his worry grew.

The colonel looked at the faint green numbering on his watch. "We've taken exactly six minutes to reach this point from the prison courtyard," he said. "If Lennox

and I aren't back at the lorry in fifteen minutes flat,
return to the camp. Remember to signal with your headlights as you approach it so that our guards will recognize
you at once. Lieutenant Simmins, check the time." The
two officers compared their wrist watches. There was a
tightening in the faces of the waiting men.

Johann moved impatiently, and the colonel slowly left
the lorry's shadow. Lennox, at a sign, followed with equal
reluctance. Johann was leading them into the wood by a
well-marked path, so carefully cleared of trees and
branches that Lennox realized it was as well used as it
was marked. It was only the black blanket of night,
smothering recognizable shapes and distorting them into
ominous shadows, which made this small wood seem so
mysterious and dangerous. In daylight it would probably
seem a very simple and innocent place.

When they had traveled less than a hundred yards (at
first slowly, then more surely as their eyes became accustomed to the depths of shadows around them) and found
themselves in a clearing Lennox knew his guess had been
accurate enough. The path had been merely the entrance
to a beer garden. For in the clearing before him were
wooden tables and benches, and beyond these lay a two-
storied wooden house built in the Tyrolese manner with
broad eaves overshadowing its side walls. An inn. That's
what it would be: a nice, woodland place for a picnic
or a family reunion.

A family reunion. Lennox's lips tightened, and he
stared at the chalet, still and shuttered, lit only by the
clear stars which shone so brightly above the clearing.

The colonel had halted too, but he was watching
Johann. "Is this the place?" he asked.

Johann nodded. He was already walking over the
stretch of soft, fine grass towards the house. He motioned
impatiently with his hand for them to follow.

"Stay here," the colonel said quietly, grasping Lennox
suddenly by the arm. "Keep in the shadows. I'll do the

bargaining. I think I'm getting the hang of the boy's dialect now. If I need you I'll call you. If I meet trouble I'll fire a shot. Then you will get back to the lorry and tell them to make for the camp at once. All quite clear?"

"If you are expecting trouble, sir, then I'd better——"

"No. You get back to the lorry to warn them." The colonel's voice was gloomy. His thin face was white under the starlight, but there was a determined cheerfulness in the smile he gave Lennox. Somehow it depressed Lennox still more. But his resentment against the colonel was disappearing. He was beginning to understand the colonel. He was even beginning to feel sorry for him.

Lennox settled back into the shadow of a group of trees, watched the tall, thin figure hurry after Johann, and then stared at the wood around him. "Rather he than I," Lennox said to himself, as the officer followed Johann into the inn. He thought of the colonel's gaunt white face, lined with perpetual anxieties, tight-lipped and cold-eyed with worry. That's what responsibility did to a man. You could never make a decision without worrying whether it was the best one; you could never refuse a possibility without thinking of a lost opportunity. Whichever way you chose, you worried. Now the colonel was probably beginning to wish he hadn't started on this plan of Johann's. And yet, as Lennox waited, more nervously than he was willing to admit, he couldn't see what else the colonel should have done. For the men in the prison camp had little chance as matters stood now: they hadn't enough arms, they had wounded among them who couldn't travel or fight, they didn't know much about the countryside. The only alternative, as far as Lennox could see, would be for the band of prisoners to scatter and to look out each for himself. That would have been all right for Lennox or any who had been planning escape, but the others wouldn't have much of a chance. And if they were captured then there would be no chance

at all for them. The dead Germans in the little castle, up
there on the hill behind him, would decide that.

Lennox stared at the wood's shadows around him. He
stared at the door of the silent chalet. He stared at
the faintly glowing numbers on his wrist watch. He held
the revolver in the German coat pocket so tightly that
his weakened hand grew quite numb. Six minutes, eight
minutes. He shifted his weight and tautened as a twig
broke under his foot. Eleven minutes. The door opened
at last. He raised the revolver slowly, supporting his hand
with his left fist. The colonel was there all right. And
Johann. And two other men—young men by their easy
stride. As the group approached him he could see the
strangers were wearing the usual dress of the South
Tyrol—leather breeches, light-colored wool stockings,
shapeless felt hats, tweed jackets.

Lennox could see by the way the men walked that
much had been decided. It didn't need the colonel's
quiet "Everything laid on" to tell him that it had been
thoroughly decided.

As they left the clearing to plunge into the wood the
colonel was saying, "These chaps have already moved all
guns and ammunition from the barracks—they knew the
Germans would occupy it as soon as the railway was
secured. The guns have been hidden in this wood, and
these men are going to help us load the lorry with what
it can hold. They say they've enough ammunition, too.
They will take care of our wounded, and shelter them
until they are strong enough to follow us. They will give
us guides to help us by-pass the German troops in this
valley. After that we fight on our own to the south. If we
move quickly enough we have a sporting chance to reach
the Allied front before the Germans can reinforce the
gaps which the Italians left in their defense lines. God
knows where our front will be before we reach it; it may
be in Rome and moving northwards before the month
is out if the Italians really rise up against the Germans.

But wherever they are we'll make a stab at finding them. We can't go far wrong if we keep going south."

Lennox said nothing for a full minute. Everything was settled, then; as fully settled as it could be. The men up in the castle had now, at least, a fighting chance. Sporting was the word that the colonel had used. Fighting would be nearer the truth. After his years of experience with the Italians Lennox wasn't so sure that the Allies' path to Rome would be made easy for them. He was willing to bet that the colonel had not been fighting long in the Mediterranean theater. The colonel still believed in the milk of human kindness.

"What's the guarantee of good faith, sir?" he asked quietly. These Tyrolese had given too much without demanding something in return.

"You are. You are going up there with the boy, Johann." The colonel pointed northeast where the black mass of jagged peaks rose beyond the River Eisak. "There is a plateau up there which they call the Schlern. You will stay there, keeping your ears and eyes well open, until some of our men can be dropped in to join you."

Lennox stared through the darkness. The colonel must have felt his amazement, for he said quickly, "When we reach the Allied lines we'll get Intelligence onto the job. They'll send some of their men by parachute onto the Schlern to join you. We'll build up something there that will jolt the Huns."

Lennox thought of several observations to make on such optimism, but none seemed suitable to a superior officer. He said, more quietly than he felt, "Very good, sir."

The men round the lorry listened to the colonel's instructions. Below them the lights in the town pinpricked the darkness. The three Tyrolese stood quietly competent, eagerly ready. Everything was, as the colonel had first said, everything was laid on.

The lorry had started back up the hill with its load of

men and guns. ("Enough," the colonel had said, "enough for a starter, anyway. We'll collect more on our way south.")

Johann touched Lennox's arm. The Englishman was watching the crawling truck, already part of the night's blackness. Then he turned to follow the boy. To the northeast the mountains were still as remote and fantastic as they had seemed to Lennox staring at them through the barbed wire of a prison camp. Then they had been remote and fantastic because they had symbolized freedom. Now they themselves had become a prison, from which there was no escape. And he was walking into that prison, if not willingly then certainly without a revolver at his back.

"Why do you laugh?" Johann asked curiously. "It isn't wise to laugh yet. We are too near these houses. Tomorrow, up on the Schlern, you can laugh all you want to."

Lennox was suddenly serious. "Yes, I'll laugh then," he said grimly. He followed the boy's sure steps, and wondered how many weeks it would take his comrades to reach the Allied lines. But he didn't let himself think of the feeling they would have when they could be back with their own people again.

Johann's quiet voice held its own revolt. "I had other plans too, for tonight," he was saying, almost reprovingly. "My girl is down in Bozen, and when I don't turn up to see her as I promised she will start worrying about the stray bullets which were flying this afternoon. And I don't know whether she is safe either. She is not the kind to stay home and hide under the bed. So," his voice sharpened, "let's start moving."

Lennox thought how easy it was to forget that other people had their own private worries and disappointments. To appease this sudden twinge of conscience, he said politely, "Is she from the Tyrol too?"

"Eva?" Johann asked quickly, and by that quickness and that pleased note in his voice he showed that he wanted the other's friendship. "Yes, she's from my village. Now she is living in Bozen with relatives." The boy talked on, quickly, interminably—about his village, which had been called Montefierro for the last twenty-four years, but which now reverted to the name of Hinterwald that had suited it very well for over three hundred years; about Eva Mussner.

Lennox followed him obediently, imitating his short plodding step up the steep incline of hillside. But Lennox said nothing at all. He began to regret his simple question. The friendly warmth in this boy's voice beat against the cold wall which imprisonment had built round his emotions. He learned to live within himself. Miller's death tonight only proved that affection and human liking brought deeper sorrow. The man who lived alone could laugh at life and tell it to do its damnedest. That way, a man was less vulnerable. What he wouldn't allow himself to enjoy, he couldn't be afraid of losing. Lennox stopped listening to Johann; his uneasiness turned to resentment. Hell, he thought irritably, what's this Hinterwald or Eva Mussner to me? He scarcely noticed when the boy's mumbling words grew farther spaced, and the sudden burst of confidence became a frozen block of silence.

Far to the south of them came a sudden burst of rifle fire. Lennox halted instinctively and looked back. It wasn't an attack on the prison camp, for the machine guns, now firing heavily, were down in the valley.

Johann pulled his arm impatiently. "It is only the Germans and some angry Italians shooting it out," he said. "And that will be good for your friends. The Germans have many worries tonight."

Lennox watched the distant flashes of light, the sudden flaring of some ammunition or petrol dump. It was not an unpleasant feeling to turn his back on the skirmishing, to walk away into the darkness and leave those who had killed and mutilated so many of his friends now tearing at one another like the traitors in Dante's hell.

CHAPTER 7

The Schlern is really the highest of a group of mountains in the Dolomite Alps, but its name has come also to mean the high plateau of rolling meadows and forests over which the steep face of this rocky mass rises like some enormous fortress.

The road up to the Schlern begins in the Eisak Valley, which leads southward to Italy and northward through the Brenner Pass to Austria. The road ascends steeply, by sudden twists and sharp turns. It cuts through cliffs of rock by narrow tunnels; it holds precariously to the precipice edge; it arrives at last—much to the relief of the traveler—on what seems to be the top of the world. But relief gives way to amazement, for up here lies still another world; one of villages and scattered farms and churches, of winding roads and streams and green meadows, of forests and mountain peaks challenging to still greater height. This is the Schlernland, an island of Alpine scenery pushed into the sky. It isn't a naked, jutting kind of island, for the deep valleys surrounding it have their rugged waves of mountains too. On every side the sea of precipices is unending.

Perhaps it was because this road up to the Schlern was so treacherous in winter, or because the Germans found they had enough to worry about in keeping open the supply route in the Eisak Valley, that the Schlern had had one of its most peaceful winters. The Italian policemen, postmasters, soldiers, schoolteachers, and hotel owners had gone. The skiers had not come this winter, just as the mountain climbers had been absent last summer. The larger chalets and villas, which the wealthy Italians from Rome and Milan had built to give their children pleasant holidays, were now as empty as the small cottages abandoned by those Tyrolese who had listened to Hitler in 1939, and had moved into Austria. The people of the Schlern who had clung to their heritage, who had refused to put their trust in politicians' promises, called themselves—with their own grim smile—the survivors.

The winter had been hard. High on the Schlern a thick frozen blanket of snow had covered the gray peaks and the green slopes. The small villages, the scattered houses of forester and farmer, had fallen into a seeming sleep among the white mountains. Down in the valley below the Schlern, where the gap in the Dolomite highlands led north to the Brenner Pass, there were snow and sleet and cruel winds to huddle the people into their houses. There were other reasons, too. The Germans had taken possession: their soldiers patrolled through alternating ice and slush, as they guarded the railway line and the flow of supplies to the German armies in Italy. German edicts, German puppets, controlled the towns on the railway line. Allied bombing planes attacked them. Far to the south, in Italy, there were driving rain and earth so sodden that the fighting fronts churned into delaying mud. The hope that October had brought had become as frozen as the earth from which the Dolomite Alps rose so steeply. The winter had been hard.

In the houses high on the Schlern it was whispered that the Allies couldn't approach the Brenner until autumn now. Perhaps not even then. This spring would come too quickly to be of any use to people who waited four hundred miles north of the Allied lines. But hope was like the earth: it was frozen, but it was not dead. The old men, the gaunt-cheeked women, the remaining young men (who had escaped from the recruiting interest of any German ski patrol by vanishing into the thick pine

forests which fringed the mountains' base), didn't talk
very much. But they had their own thoughts. They listened in to the forbidden Allied broadcasts, and they
were making their decisions. Here was a third group of
foreigners who would come to invade the Dolomites.
Would they be like the Italians or the Germans, who,
once they came to a country, claimed possession? Or
were these foreigners, who called themselves "The Allies,"
different? Were they really fighting for other peoples' freedom as well as their own? After twenty-five years of
Italian domination the people on the Schlern, like all the
Tyrolese on the other Dolomite slopes, were waiting for
the autumn of 1944. If it couldn't be this spring which
would end this waiting then let it be the autumn. It was
more than a hope; in many hearts it had become a prayer.

The people went about their daily tasks as if there were
no war. But they measured their food carefully, they listened eagerly to the radio, they hid their men from the
German patrols, they pretended ignorance in reply to all
the regulations and proclamations of the newly named
"Alpenvorland." They never forgot that in the village of
Kastelruth at the edge of the Schlern, where the road
from the valley below came to rest on a gentle green
slope, there was a token German garrison. They never
forgot that these armed foreigners were there, not to give
them a feeling of "protection," as the Germans said in
the best gangster fashion, but to police the Schlern plateau and keep it under informal observation.

The Germans didn't expect trouble. The people of
the South Tyrol were Austrians, after all. And Austria
was now a part of Greater Germany. So the garrison was
small, and its periodic patrols were less thorough as the
winter severity increased. And if the Tyrolese up on this
plateau had shown no response to the February procla-
mation, that all men between eighteen and fifty-five years
of age must report to the German Military Headquarters
in Bozen, then the Germans at Kastelruth blamed that on

the slow and stubborn nature of the highlander. They would deal with him, once the more accessible districts of the South Tyrol had been brought into line. The Germans were quite content to play a waiting game.

But the peace of the mountains is a deceiving thing: the impassive face of the highlander is equally baffling. Neither the mountains nor the people who live among them are as simple as they look.

CHAPTER 8

Peter Lennox watched the pools of green grass appear through the melting slush. With the same impatience, he had watched the first blanket of snow on the Schlern. But now there was a bitter feeling of failure added to the impatience, turning its edge to knife-sharp disappointment. The inactivity of the long winter months frayed his nerves. The people who had sheltered him had been decent and kind. He would admit that. But their very quietness, their acceptance of the fact that no message had come from any Allied Command, only added to his sense of failure. He had helped no one. He had been of no use to anyone. And the colonel and Jock and Ferry and all the others— whose names were even beginning to fade from his memory (he could only remember those of his fellow prisoners whom he had either liked or disliked very much)—had been either captured or killed. For that must be the explanation of this silence. There could be no other reason: that damned colonel couldn't have meant him to sit up here all winter, watching the snow clouds bank against a string of rocky teeth. Or could he have? When they had parted eight months ago down on the roadway outside of Bozen the colonel had talked of action, of urgent necessity. Action . . . urgent necessity—sugar-coating on a bitter pill, so that his inflated pride would let him swallow his disappointment about being left up here among a lot of women and boys and old men.

And now it was May. The last blot of snow had soaked into the sodden fields. Lennox had made up his mind.

As he dressed in the small room which had become so familiar—with its narrow window tucked under the broad overhanging roof, with its carved wooden bed and thick soft mattress, with its one small table and chair, and white scrubbed floor—he was rehearsing the speech he would make.

"Frau Schichtl!" he would say. "What's the use of staying here any longer? The plan, which your highly esteemed brother in Bozen made, has definitely not come off. The only sensible thing now—begging your esteemed brother's pardon, for he seems a most determined man— is for me to leave your house and end the worry you've had ever since Johann brought me here. I had a plan for escape, and I haven't forgotten it. I'll reach the Allied lines. And I'll tell the Whosits all about you here on the Schlern. I'll tell them about the man from Bozen whom I have never met, and about the hatchet-faced old boys, who come on a Saturday evening to drink your home-made wine around the kitchen table and talk and talk and talk. And the Whosits will send the right men up here. Men who will talk and talk and talk, and feel perfectly happy becaue they know what they are doing. They won't have guilt every time they look at the mattress on a most comfortable bed; and they'll have so many plans inside their specially trained brains that they won't mind sitting in a room all day and every day. They enjoy hiding. That's part of their job. And they'll be really helpful. They'll parachute all over this place." He paused while he crossed over to the window to shut out the cold morning air.

"You are getting soft," he told himself angrily. "Now, where were you?" He stared at himself truculently in the small square of mirror. He saw a white-faced young man with even features, and strong eyebrows now drawn together in a bad-tempered frown. His hair was too long, his chin needed a shave. The gray eyes were clear and direct, but their look was hard enough to jolt him away

from the mirror. He didn't like his looks. He picked up
the loose jacket of gray tweed and pulled it over his white
shirt and black waistcoat as he started to descend the
bare staircase. His heavy shoes, lowcut, ugly and strong,
struck angrily on the white-scrubbed wood. He slowed
up, and set his feet down more quietly. In the kitchen
below was a bright wood fire in a neat stove, the smell
of newly baked bread, the early sun streaming through
the small window, and Frau Schichtl.

She poured out a cup of new milk as she heard him
leaving the room upstairs, and she was now measuring
the careful spoonfuls of homemade jam onto his plate. The
newly baked bread was wrapped in its white cloth on the
dresser: on the table was a staler loaf. (New bread was
too uneconomical; it sliced extravagantly and was eaten
too quickly.) The rough linen cloth on the table was
clean; the large white coarse cups were clean; the room
was clean. Everything was neat and clean, from the well-
scrubbed face and well-brushed hair of Frau Schichtl to
the stiff little curtains of white lace above the precise row
of ivy pots on the sill.

Lennox said a mild good-morning, and fingered his
chin nervously as he slid into his chair at the table. He
ought to have shaved after all, he thought, as he glanced
up at Frau Schichtl's quiet face. She had the same wide-
spaced blue eyes as her son, Johann. Now these eyes were
watching him curiously. He wished she would sit down.
She was almost his height, and that was tall for a woman.
Now, as she stood there so impassively, her strong arms
and capable hands flowing from her broad shoulders, her
well-shaped head erect on the long, firm neck, he felt as
young as Johann. He resented it. And that gave him
courage.

"Frau Schichtl!" he began. "Frau Schichtl, what's the
use of—"

But she had turned her back towards the door and was

listening to something else. He watched the decided curve
of jaw and the line of high cheekbone in profile.

"Anything wrong?" he asked.

"No. I only thought I heard Johann. He came home
at dawn today. He's asleep now. He had a long journey
this time." She moved suddenly to the entrance hall,
which formed the sitting room of the house, and stood
listening at the foot of the staircase. He could see her,
the tall, strong figure in its severe black dress, intent on
listening. The beams of light from the kitchen and sitting-
room windows made a good angle against the soft background of darkened pine walls. The still darker furniture
formed solid shapes, bright surfaced with polishing, so
that they held the glancing light. Interior, he thought, interior in the Dutch manner. And then he glanced down
at his right hand. Frau Schichtl, coming back into the
kitchen with her slow, even step, saw the bitter smile on
his lips. She forgot about Johann.

"What is it, Peter?" she asked quickly.

Lennox's right hand slid under the table. He lifted the
heavy cup of milk with his left hand. He didn't want to
test the right hand now, not with Frau Schichtl's sharp
blue eyes watching him.

"What news does Johann bring?" he countered.

"A lot. About many things." She stopped watching him
and moved suddenly over to the oven. She unwrapped
the white cloth which lay on its side ledge. She picked
up a loaf and cut a thick slice with its floury golden crust
still warm.

"Try this," she said, and offered him the new bread.

Lennox stared at her in surprise. He took the bribe
with almost a smile. But Frau Schichtl was now too pre-
occupied with her own thoughts even to notice it.

"Why don't you like us?" she asked suddenly, staring
at the floor in front of his feet.

Lennox moved restlessly. "I do like you," he said very
evenly. "You have been very kind."

"Yet you are not happy. If you really liked us then you would be happy."

"That doesn't follow."

She raised her eyes and studied his face with a puzzled look. "You want to leave," she said at last. "You think this a prison." It was a statement, rather than a challenge, and she said it so sadly that Lennox found himself answering. He tried to keep the irritation out of his voice, but his words were tight and hard.

"That," he said, "is a fact about me, and not about you or about the people of those mountains out there." He nodded towards the window. "You've all been kind. You've given me as much food as you've had for yourself. Sometimes more. You've given me shelter. You've hidden me well. I understand why I can't leave this house through the day, why I've got to stay upstairs most of the time. I understand why the neighboring houses aren't even supposed to know I am here. I understand why no one sees me except you, and Johann, and the local Committee who come up to visit you once a week. Your brother who lives in Bozen has provided excellent identification papers proving I am your nephew from the North Tyrol. The story is plausible, I know: I came here this winter, after being discharged from the German army, and the wounds I got in North Africa keep me close to this house. You've done your best for me. I know all that. But I also know your risk is greater than mine. I'll lose one life if I am caught. But you'll lose everything— Johann's life, your friends' lives, this house, everything. So, Frau Schichtl, I know this isn't a prison. But I still feel a prisoner. That's a fact about me."

Frau Schichtl said slowly, "I don't understand." She passed a flat hand over the side of her brow, smoothing the soft curls at the temple into the heavy sleekness of her hair.

"I am not a prisoner of your friends," Lennox said gently, "I'm a prisoner of events."

"But so are we."

He shook his head impatiently. "My job for eight months has amounted to sitting here and doing nothing. That's a fine way, I must say, to fight a war."

"But that wasn't your fault. Or ours. We've been waiting, like you, for instructions. We could act, all of us, but we might do the wrong things. We might bring the Germans down on us like an avalanche, and then we never could do anything. Then, when we *were* needed, we would be unable to help. Don't you see, Peter, we've got to wait until we get the right orders?"

"But we may never get them. Something's gone wrong. The Allies don't even know we are waiting for one small sign from them."

"Surely—" Frau Schichtl began, and then stopped. The lines at the side of her mouth deepened. Her eyelids drooped as if to hide the hurt look in her eyes. Suddenly she came to life again. She shrugged her shoulders, and there was a difficult smile on her lips.

"I know," she said, in a low voice. "I've thought of all of that too." And as Lennox stared at her in amazement, she began to straighten the tablecloth, smoothing off the crumbs of bread into her cupped hand. Then she laid two plates neatly opposite each other, and two cups for milk. For a moment he wondered if she had waited to eat breakfast with Johann. And then he saw that she was lifting the kerchief and green cape which hung on one of the wooden pegs near the door. She was leaving, as she did each morning, for the small school down in the village of Hinterwald. Last autumn Frau Schichtl had volunteered to become a teacher again. The Italian teachers had gone, and Frau Schichtl had taken over the job of keeping the school open. That, as she had explained with one of her infrequent smiles, at least prevented a stranger from coming into the Hinterwald to teach—a stranger sent by the Germans. Now she was gathering together the textbooks she had studied last night and the notebook in which she had so carefully prepared today's lessons. Her pupils would have been amused at the home-work which their new teacher had to do.

"Who has come here with Johann?" Lennox asked, looking pointedly at the two cups on the table.

Frau Schichtl's thoughts came back into the small room. She said quickly, "I meant to tell you. It's my brother. He has some special news for you, and for the others."

"The man from Bozen," Lennox said softly. "So he's here." He smiled, and then he began to laugh.

Frau Schichtl looked at him almost sadly. "That's the first time I've heard you laugh," she said, "and I don't know why you are laughing."

"I was thinking what a fine soldier I've become. I didn't even hear your brother or Johann arrive. I'd have done just as well if they had been a couple of Germans."

"In that case," Frau Schichtl said, "I would have found a way of wakening you." She didn't say, as she might well have done, "Please don't think that everything is perfectly normal and safe just because I try to give the appearance of being normal and unworried. Don't think that, young man."

Peter Lennox rose and went towards the door of the kitchen. "I'll get back to my room," he said. Rules of the house. When Frau Schichtl went out he had to stay upstairs with the bedroom door locked. Then he added, "I'm sorry. I've worried you. I never thought you did worry, because you always look so calm. If I had known your brother was here I would have kept my remarks for him." He touched her awkwardly on the shoulder. She smiled suddenly, and the lines of her mouth were no longer tired or unhappy.

She moved slowly towards the entrance door. "Perhaps I should have told you more this winter," she said, "and then you wouldn't have worried because you thought there was nothing to worry about."

Lennox had no answer to that. He began to climb the stairs. He was glad, unexpectedly, that he hadn't made the speech he had prepared. He ought to have remembered that women, no matter where they came from or what language they spoke, always had the last word. Never argue with a woman, he thought: it's a waste of good breath. When he reached the small square landing he heard the entrance door open and then shut. The heavy sounds seemed to tell him that the conversation in the kitchen—as far as Frau Schichtl was concerned—was equally closed. Even the way a woman shut a door could be her last word. He smiled in spite of himself.

CHAPTER 9

He loitered in the darkness of the upper hall for some moments, wondering in which room Johann and his uncle were sleeping. This wooden house was solidly built: he could hear nothing. The silence oppressed him. He moved quickly into his own room, and, out of habit, twisted the clumsy key in its iron lock.

From the window, shielded by the white starched curtain from outside eyes, he could see Frau Schichtl making her way carefully round the pools of heavy mud. The road to Hinterwald was scarcely more than a cart track. It served as a link between Hinterwald and these outlying houses, and as a short cut over the wooded hillside to the next village. A better but longer road twisted through the meadows farther to the west. It was the "foreigners' road," Frau Schichtl had said. But whether that meant it was built by foreigners or used by foreigners, Lennox didn't know. At least, the Germans didn't use this cart track. The Schichtl house, and the Kasal farmhouse some fifty yards away, might have been a hundred miles from anywhere. Lennox could have counted on one hand the number of strangers whom he had watched passing in the last eight months.

The Kasals' eldest daughter was waiting at the doorway of the farmhouse as usual. Her yellow hair gleamed in the early morning sunlight as she ran to join Frau Schichtl. The girl was laughing. Her bare feet and legs ploughed carelessly through the spring mud. Her shoes were held safely together in one hand, her school books were in the other. He envied her the freedom with which she could walk and laugh. He opened the window carefully, slowly. The fresh air brought the smell of grass and rain, of pine trees and free mountain winds into his small room. He had an impulse to lean out of the window and feel the touch of the early morning sun on his face. But he stayed dutifully behind the white screens, under the broad, overhanging eaves, and looked at the green alp sloping gently down towards the village.

The Kasal house was silent now. Smoke was trickling placidly from its wide stone chimney. Its broad roof was safely anchored against winter storms by large stones roped together. The bright blue shutters, whitened at the seams, needed their spring coat of paint. The pile of logs under the ground-floor windows had grown small. Soon the woodcutters would need to go to work in the forest. The window boxes on the carved wooden balcony, which ran across the front of the house, waited for their load of flowers. The five gaunt cows had been allowed into the highest field today and were guarded there by the Kasals' dog, so that they would not wander into the lower pastures, which were still waterlogged. From across the fields Lennox could hear Alois Kasal's voice giving encouragement and commands, and the sound of the harness bells on the plow horse as it obeyed him. Spring, Lennox thought, and hope was stirring everywhere. The dead sleep of winter was gone. Now he knew the reason for his mounting bitterness: when it was the time for hope, and you knew that there could be no hope, you became bitter. He hated everyone and everything in that moment. Most of all, he hated himself.

He looked at his watch. It was now eight o'clock in the morning. At two o'clock Frau Schichtl would be home and would start preparing dinner. At five o'clock they would have their one meal of the day. At seven o'clock they would sit around the kitchen oven. Frau Schichtl would go over her work for school next day. Lennox

would practice drawing with his stupid left hand, and
wonder bitterly if ever it could be taught to obey his mind.
At eight o'clock they would try to hear the news from Allied broadcasts. They would strain to catch a small piece
of information through the constant background of interference. And then, if the weather were good and the moon
was weak, Lennox would take a short walk towards the
pine forest at the back of the house. Or more often, when
the weather was so bad that it was dangerous to move outside, he would stand in the shadows of the opened back
door with a darkened room behind him, and stare into
the freezing, wind-swept night. He would lose his thoughts
in the swaying mass of pine branches, in the hard resolute
face of rocky peaks which rise behind the forest's crest.
He would wait until the blood in his veins froze with the
cold mountain air in spite of the green *loden* cape round
his shoulders. He would wait until his hope was frozen,
too. (No one was coming: this mission was useless. He
was wasting his time, losing his energy, bringing danger
on this house and its neighbors. And each month his
maimed right hand became gradually and steadily more
helpless, as if the old wound were now paying him out
for the perfunctory treatment it had been given in a prison
camp.) Then, before nine o'clock, Frau Schichtl would
stand shivering behind him, prodding him on the spine
until he turned back into the house and closed the door,
barring it, shutting out another day of his life. At nine
o'clock the lights were extinguished, the oven fire was
carefully banked for the night, and he would lie in this
lonely room, listening to the roof's strange groans and
the uncanny noises of the wooden walls. At first he used
to think they were the sounds of movement outside the
house, and he would rise quickly to stand beside the cold
window. But now his alarms had vanished with his hopes,
and he no longer leaped out of bed in anxiety of expec-
tation. Now he expected exactly nothing.

For a moment he hesitated, his eyes still on his watch. What should he do today? He could read the books he already knew by heart. He could straighten the bed and put things into order. He could practice some more left-handed writing on the few precious pieces of paper he had borrowed from Frau Schichtl's school notebook. He could do some physical exercises, which was the only way he kept his muscles firm. He could slump on the bed and memorize once more the things he had learned in the last months. Or he could slump on the bed and think of the old days. Or he could slump on the bed. After eight months these suggestions had lost all variety. He went over them nonchalantly, and was no longer amazed that his thinking was not done in English but in the Austrian dialect of the Tyrol. He had started this habit about Christmas, so that he would really learn the language. Now it seemed the natural way to express his thoughts. He wasn't laughing any more, either, at the strange place names of the Schlern. If only Dusty Miller had been here with him, or big Jock . . . someone to talk to. Someone who would not always be polite. Someone who'd argue with you. Someone who'd see the joke in everyday names. "Puflatsch, Bad Ratzes, Eggen-Tal," he said aloud, but he didn't even smile now. Miller could have woven half an hour's conversation out of them and raised a dozen laughs. Lennox could have done that too—once.

"Time I was getting out of here, and getting out pretty damn quick," he said emphatically. Now that the man from Bozen was here it would be easier to give his ultimatum. It hadn't been so easy with Frau Schichtl. Three times now, upstairs in this room, he had made the resolution that he was leaving. Three times, downstairs, his resolution had melted away. Somehow a woman always made you feel a swine if you insisted on doing something she didn't want you to do. Today, it was true, he had begun to say what was on his mind. He smiled, remembering the way in which the door had closed.

"Five minutes past eight," he said. He talked aloud quite a lot now. Well, he had certainly used up five minutes of this day. He looked down at the roadway, and wondered how slow it would be to travel through roads as mud-filled as that. The ground was thawing out now, and the water from the melting snow on the mountains streamed down onto the meadows. But Frau Schichtl had said it drained off quickly. She had said the higher fields and woods were already passable. If Johann would guide him by the secret paths known to those who had been brought up in this district the journey would be much simpler. And once he was out of this chain of mountains he could strike, alone, southeast across the plains. He could reach the Adriatic and Jugoslavia this time. His plans to reach them were still as fresh in his mind as they had been eight months ago.

He stiffened. He stood motionless, his eyes rigid. On the road, slipping heavily on the yellowish mud, were two figures. They were walking towards Hinterwald. They hesitated as they neared the house, halted beside a tree. The taller figure seemed to be urging the other on. They started again towards the house. The uncertain one was limping now. He was leaning heavily on his friend's shoulder.

Lennox moved quickly. He was out of his room, and he was knocking sharply on all the three doors on the landing before he had even got his thoughts straight. From one door came Johann's voice, and then a deeper voice asking, "What the devil?"

It was Johann who appeared. His sleepy eyes opened fully as Lennox pushed past him to confront the bearded man who was sitting up in bed.

"Two men are approaching this house," Lennox was saying. "American flyers, I think. One of you had better get downstairs and put out the Welcome mat."

"What the devil—" the bearded man began. He rubbed the back of his head and yawned widely. But he was reaching for his trousers lying over the rail at the foot of the bed. "I'll go," he grumbled. He glanced at his large silver watch on the chair beside him. "Three hours' sleep. Hand me those boots, damn you. Thanks. So you are Lennox? I'm Paul Mahlknecht. Johann, stand by. If I call come downstairs. Lennox, you stay up here."

Lennox nodded. Paul Mahlknecht was already hurrying out of the room, buttoning his trousers with one hand, slipping his broad bright-colored braces over his shoulders with the other. He lifted his waistcoat from the chair as he kicked the door open. He gave Lennox a rueful shake of his head as he left the room. "No rest these days," he said, with considerable enjoyment.

Downstairs the front door was opening. There was the sound of heavy, dragging footsteps.

"Anyone here?" a strange voice called. It repeated the question in English.

Lennox stood very still. Then he crossed over to the door and closed it quietly.

"Perhaps they are *your* friends," Johann said, with his broad, simple smile.

"Perhaps." Lennox was too tense. He walked over to the window. This time he was looking from the back of the house, over to the pine woods, up to the mountains. This was the view he had seen each night as he had waited for someone who had never come. Now they had come. He couldn't believe it.

"Perhaps," he said again, trying to fight down his emotion.

CHAPTER 10

Johann was talking as he dressed. He was half grumbling, half pleased. "Another journey," he was saying. "I've just finished taking three Americans into Jugoslavia. God, can't they give a man some rest?"

Peter Lennox smiled at that. He turned from the window to look at the "man." The boy's face was hidden by a rough towel as he polished his red-apple cheeks.

"So that's what you've been doing in these last months," Lennox said. He realized now why Johann had kept silent about such a job. Lennox would have wanted to go along too.

"That's what I've been doing." Pride was in Johann's voice. "Personal escort service." He threw the towel at Lennox, and began pulling on his shirt.

"Meet any trouble?"

"It's getting more difficult," Johann acknowledged. "The first batches were easy. The Germans never guessed we would help any Allied flyers. But now the remains of several planes have been found in the South Tyrol, without a live American or Britisher to show for them. So the Germans are beginning to wonder. No grounded flyer could make his way alone out of these mountains unless he were an expert climber and had a mountaineering map. He would have to come down into the valleys and ask for help. Now the Germans are increasing their garrisons and patrols. They are in a nasty temper about that, too." The smile had left Johann's face. Watching him, Lennox suddenly realized that Johann was no longer a boy. But then, journeys over and around these Dolomite peaks in winter would age anyone. Death lay waiting at many a twisting corner in a mountain path.

"And how have you been?" Johann's politeness was formal. He was really listening for any possible call from downstairs. When Lennox gave no answer to that he went on cheerily, "Got to keep an ear cocked, you know." But his eyes were thoughtful and he was watching the Englishman.

"What you need is some exercise," Johann said suddenly. "Perhaps it wouldn't be a bad idea if you started some mountain climbing too, soon."

"Perhaps I shall," Lennox said grimly.

Johann was still watching him, as if he could read the meaning behind the short words. "I don't blame you," he said at last. "Being shut up in this house would drive me crazy. But you can't tell that to my mother, though." He laughed and then stopped short. He opened the door slightly. It was Mahlknecht, calling in very definite terms for both of them to hurry up and come downstairs.

"Both of us?" Lennox asked, and there was a first real note of gladness in his voice. His hope had grown to a certainty.

Johann pushed him good-naturedly out of the room towards the staircase. "Let Uncle Paul set the pace," he whispered, "Cousin Peter from the North Tyrol." He was grinning widely. Lennox was smiling too as they clattered down the wooden stairs.

In the sitting room there were mud-caked footsteps on the floor, and two pairs of heavy flying boots lying side by side. That must have been the point where Paul Mahlknecht had stopped the two strangers and made them take off their boots. Frau Schichtl's rules were observed even by the formidable brother from Bozen, it seemed.

Mahlknecht had chosen to remain standing. The two flyers were sitting on the hard wooden bench against the

wall near the stove. They were huddling towards the heat
of its wood fire. On the seat the light from the two kitchen
windows fell sharply across their faces. Their eyes looked
up as Johann and Lennox entered.

Mahlknecht said, "One of them speaks a little German.
The other doesn't. They don't seem to understand me
very well."

Lennox, conscious of the strangers' eyes watching
Johann and him curiously, kept his face emotionless. But
the tide of hope which had surged through his heart only
a minute ago suddenly ebbed. These men hadn't come
seeking him. They had obviously not even asked for him;
and they couldn't even talk German properly. The men
who would be sent must certainly be able to talk and
understand the Austrian dialect of the Tyrol. And then
Lennox was conscious of another thing: Mahlknecht,
whose voice upstairs had held less accent than Johann's,
was now using the coarsest form of dialect. Words were
slurred, endings were altered, some consonants were elim-
inated, vowels were broadened to the point of caricature.
Lennox had to strain to catch the meaning of these three
sentences. And a signal seemed to have been given to
Johann. He stopped lounging, drew his hands out of the
pockets of his trousers, and decided not to sit at the table
as he had intended. He strolled carelessly over to one of
the windows, and leaned against the broad sill with his
back to the light. Lennox chose a chair in the darkest
corner of the kitchen, between Johann and the door. It
was then that he wondered why Paul Mahlknecht should
have called him downstairs along with Johann. Unless
these men had been sent to make contact with him, it was
dangerous and stupid to bring him down here. But the
dark, bearded face of Mahlknecht with its broad brow,
deep-set and thoughtful eyes gave no answer. And something in the rich, deep calmness of this man showed his
strength and will and judgment. Peter Lennox sat back
in his chair. He was watching the two strangers now. If

he had been brought down here then there was some reason. He would have to find it.

"Does no one speak English?" the taller of the two strangers asked. He spoke slowly in German, looking anxiously at Johann and then at Lennox. He was a dark-haired, broad-shouldered man with irregular features. The other had a charming, pretty-boy look, with fair hair and a delicate cut to the bones of his face. His light gray eyes were quite blank of expression, as if he had come to the end of his resistance. He would be a tiger among the girls, Lennox thought, but this was definitely not one of his better moments.

Mahlknecht drew a deeply curved pipe from his pocket. He concentrated on lighting it. His eyes met Lennox's. There was a single urgent message in them. Then they fell to watching a briefly flaring strand of tobacco. He packed the smoking bowl more tightly with his thumb, and then took a long pull at the yellowed pipe. Lennox wanted to smile: this was the treatment with a vengeance. He had been given the same long silences, the same pauses between question and answer, when he had first come here. The only difference was that he had been offered something to smoke, something to eat and drink. The only difference. . . . Lennox sat motionless in the shadowy corner, withdrawing into the anonymity of its stillness. But his eyes were doubly watchful now, and his mind was worried.

Mahlknecht began to speak, telling Johann and Lennox that here were two American flyers who had crashed some miles away after yesterday's attack on the Brenner railway. They were the only survivors. They had walked through the night. They wanted help to take them out of these mountains.

The two flyers were watching Mahlknecht with intelligent concentration. They seemed reassured by his voice, for they leaned back against the wall as if the action was now taken out of their hands. The dark-haired man was beginning to feel warmer: he opened his lambskin-lined flying jacket, and pulled it off his shoulders. He wore a faded and worn American flyer's blouse, decorated with three medals and the insignia of captain. The fair-haired flyer followed his example. Again there was an American blouse, well-fitted and this time less worn. There were decorations along the left breast pocket, and a lieutenant's bar. Both men were lusty specimens: there was a natural glow of health on their skins, their eyes were clear and alert. The fair-haired one drew a crushed packet of American cigarettes out of his blouse pocket, and lit one with an efficient lighter. He was sitting more erect now, as if his initial exhaustion had passed. He listened in silence, his eyes watchful, while his companion spoke.

"Will you help us? We need a place to sleep, some food and drink, and a guide tonight to take us south through the mountain passes." The man's German was ungrammatical. It was slow and halting. But some vague disturbing emotion jangled an alarm in Peter Lennox's mind. The man's German was ungrammatical, but words he used were easy, colloquial words, and they were correctly pronounced. If you used words so naturally why should there be such grammatical mistakes? Why the long pauses between fluent phrases? These things didn't match.

Lennox glanced at Johann and Paul Mahlknecht. They had noticed no inconsistency in the man's speech. Johann was still watching the flyers placidly, neither believing nor disbelieving. Paul Mahlknecht drew patiently at his pipe, one hand cupping its heavy bowl, the other tucked into his belt. His brown eyes were watchful under their heavy brows, but there had been no change in his expression during this last minute. I'm imagining things, Lennox thought angrily. He hated any proof of these months of loneliness: he had become too damned jumpy, too suspicious, too bloody-well sensitive. And yet the uneasiness in his mind wouldn't leave him. Joahnn and his uncle hadn't noticed the strange unbalance in this foreigner's speech, but then they had never had to learn to speak German as a foreigner. They had grown up with the language. And Lennox, remembering his own first struggles to talk German, thought of the stilted vocabulary and the mistakes in pronunciation which went with grammatical errors and stupid pauses.

"Why did you come here?" Mahlknecht was asking slowly. He was fussing with his pipe again. It seemed as if nothing was going to hurry him. The quiet room, the quiet fields and trees beyond the windows, gave emphasis to his deliberateness. The two flyers were beginning to be restless. The blond lieutenant fingered the decorations on his chest, as if to win the three peasants' trust and sympathy. The captain began replying. He was explaining that a house near the plane crash had sheltered them yesterday, that they had been told of men who lived under the Schlern Mountain who would be able to help them, that they had walked all night with the massive peak to guide them.

Lennox was only listening to the man's voice and the way he used it. He didn't listen to the words. He was suddenly convinced that Paul Mahlknecht had called him down here to make a decision. He had been called down here to determine if these men were really American flyers. The responsibility of refusing help to possibly honest friends had been placed on him. He glanced quickly at Mahlknecht. The same short but insistent look which had been given him when he entered the room was his reply. Now he was indeed convinced: Mahlknecht needed his help; Mahlknecht was somehow doubtful; Mahlknecht depended on his being able to judge a real American when he saw one.

He could have laughed. He had known Americans. Some had been with him in the second Italian camp in which he had been imprisoned. One of them had actually made that attempted escape with him, and they had come to be pretty good friends. But how was that going to make him an expert on recognizing an American? If these two strangers had been British he couldn't have been an expert on them either. The Americans and British varied too much: it was only on the stage or screen that you found stock characteristics. If he could have talked in English he could have tried some operational slang on them. Then he might have learned something. Or he could have spoken about New York. His American friend used to talk a lot about food, about certain restaurants in New York, until Lennox almost believed that he had eaten there himself. But he couldn't speak in English. He was a peasant living near Hinterwald. He could have laughed in his frustration, but there wasn't any time for laughing. Desperately he tried to think of some way, some way to find out.

"But we know of no one who could help," Mahlknecht was saying. He was playing for time, waiting for Lennox's help. "My nephew here reports for service in Bozen this week. I myself know only the mountains which lie above us. My other nephew is ill as you can see. He was honourably discharged with wounds after having fought in Libya. There is no one here who can help you. And we know of no one who could."

It struck Lennox that, for a man who could speak little German, the captain was fairly quick at understanding dialect.

"There must be some one in this village who would help us," he said quickly. "We cannot enter the village in daylight. You could at least send your young nephew to the village for someone who will help us." The voice was pathetic in its urgency.

Lennox leaned forward. The palms of his hands were hot and damp. In German he asked, "What are these?" He pointed to the ribbons on the flyer's chest.

The captain frowned in annoyance. "Medals." He

turned towards Mahlknecht again. "We are desperate. We need—"

"What for?" Lennox asked. His was obviously a one-track mind.

"For campaigns," the flyer answered impatiently. "Please help—"

"Where?"

The two flyers exchanged bitter glances.

The captain said, pointing, "This is for Egypt and Libya, this for Tunisia, this is a D.F.C. for battle."

"Libya," Lennox said reminiscently. "I was there too. And I was in Egypt. But I got no medals, only bullet holes. Where were you in Egypt?"

The captain took a deep breath. "Everywhere."

"But there weren't airfields everywhere," Lennox said slowly, with the obstinate logic of a simple man who lived among simple people. "Where was your field? I once was in an attack near a British airfield. There were Americans there, too. That's where I got this." He held up his scarred right hand. He smiled to show that there was no ill feeling. "Perhaps you or your friends gave it to me."

The captain smiled back uneasily. "Perhaps," he said.

"Where was your airfield? The one we attacked was at Beni Jara. Did you know it? About five miles south of a place they called Himeimat. That was a big one. We fought two weeks near there. That's where I got wounded." Lennox's palms were no longer sweating. He was beginning even to enjoy himself. South of Himeimat was the ugliest piece of salt marsh where no aircraft could ever have landed. And Beni Jara was a name that had just occurred to him. It sounded good enough, he thought. In fact, it sounded damn good.

"I was stationed nearer El Alamein," the captain said. He mentioned a well-known airfield. But it seemed to Lennox that the captain wasn't quite happy about something. With a consciously pleasant smile, the captain said quickly, "But of course we knew Beni Jara. In fact, I've

refueled there. Why do you ask?" There was a touch of
steel in his voice.

"It was a dangerous place. We attacked bravely. Perhaps you did win your medal."

"Of course I did." The captain was half indignant, half
amused.

"I never won any medals," Lennox said. He looked
at the scar on his hand.

The captain sensed an advantage. He pressed it hard.
"The Germans treated the Austrians badly at Beni Jara,"
he said with sympathy. "Threw them against us in hopeless attacks. I remember my friends used to talk about
that. Don't you see that is why you must help us? We
are your friends. The Germans are enemies of both of
us." He was looking at Mahlknecht as he ended. So was
the lieutenant. It was the last appeal.

Lennox was looking too. And Mahlknecht's deep-set
eyes, hardly flickering, caught that look. He saw the slow,
careful movement of Lennox's head. He saw Lennox's
tense left hand, the knuckles folded, the thumb pointing
downward.

Mahlknecht cleared his throat. "I have already told
you that you came to the wrong place. If there is such
a house as you describe then I have never heard of it.
We cannot help you. No one can. Please go."

The two flyers stared at him. Mahlknecht's face was
still impassive, as if what he said now was exactly what
he had been saying all along.

"Go," he repeated. "You came into this house unin-
vited. Go. Or I shall walk to the village and 'phone Kastelruth that you are here."

They rose to their feet, and struggled into their flying
jackets. The captain's jaw was rigid. The fair-haired
man's lips were white-edged. Mahlknecht's quiet, determined voice was final. They knew that now. They halted
in the sitting room to pull on their cumbersome flying
boots. The three men in the kitchen watched them in si-

lence. In equal silence, the two flyers left the house. They didn't turn towards the village. They went back towards the pine woods from which they had come.

There was a drawn look on Paul Mahlknecht's face. He was knocking the ashes out of his pipe with solemn concentration.

"I hope to God that you were right," he said to Lennox.

CHAPTER 11

Frau Schichtl came home early that day. She brought a pile of textbooks and notebooks. The Kasal girl accompanied her to the door, helping her to carry the slipping load of books. The girl didn't follow Frau Schichtl indoors. She stood hesitating, speaking a few words in her quiet voice. And Frau Schichtl didn't invite her to come in. She wasn't even talking very much. All she said was, "Thank you, Katharina."

The girl spoke again, but her voice was too low for Lennox to catch the meaning of her words. All he could hear was the soft lilt of a girl's voice. It was the first girl's voice he had heard in two years. He moved to the window and watched her walking slowly towards the Kasal farm. She was older than he had thought, but perhaps that was because she was now walking gravely with her head slightly bowed. Before, he had always seen her hurrying, generally running. She was wearing her shoes, and didn't even seem to notice that the mud was ruining them. He didn't need to hear the clatter of the books, which Frau Schichtl let fall on the kitchen table, to realize something was wrong.

He turned from the window, and left the fair-haired girl with the strong young body walking over the green fields. Frau Schichtl's face was white: the bright color had gone, leaving two small pink daubs on her cheeks where the red veins were broken. Paul Mahlknecht put aside his pipe carefully.

"Well, Frieda?" he asked.

Frau Schichtl sat on the bench. She folded her hands tightly on her lap. Her lips were in a bitter line.

"No more school," she said, in a low voice.

"Yes?" Mahlknecht's quiet question urged her on.

Suddenly she was speaking again, angrily.

A man had been appointed teacher of the school. He was Heinrich Mussner, the same Mussner who had left for the North Tyrol in 1939. He had come back to Hinterwald last week. Last night Germans had come from Kastelruth. They had come to see that everybody was happy in Hinterwald. That was their story. They called a meeting to discuss how Hinterwald could be improved. The meeting became merely an intimation that as this district was now incorporated into the Reich, the school would have to be better managed. The woman volunteer must go: she had been a pupil-teacher in 1917, it was true, but that was too long ago. Someone with more recent experience must be chosen. A man must be chosen. Volunteers for the job were asked. And before the slow-moving, astounded villagers had begun to understand the meaning of this move Heinrich Mussner had volunteered. He had been accepted.

"And what teaching has he ever done?" Mahlknecht demanded.

"Seemingly he has been learning to teach in these last five years."

"Aye," her brother said grimly. "We can make a guess at what he has been learning to teach."

Frau Schichtl closed her eyes wearily. "Anyway, he's in. And I'm out. The Germans left after the meeting. But they are setting up a police station, too. German policemen are arriving tomorrow. And there is to be a German postmaster. And next week more people are returning from the North Tyrol. People like Mussner who left in 1939. They are going to run this village. I can see that."

"Mussner. . . . Well, at least we know where he stands,"
Mahlknecht said. He picked up his pipe again, and studied
the bowl thoughtful. "We are supposed to be such fools
that we really believe Mussner just happened to volunteer.
We are supposed not to see that the whole meeting was
an obvious German maneuver, so that Mussner wouldn't
seem the German choice." He smiled grimly. "And so
we would not distrust or hate him."

Frau Schichtl rose and went to the table. She began ar-
ranging her books on a shelf along the wall. "Where's
Johann?" she asked.

"I sent him to the houses of the Committee with some
information. He should be back soon."

"Anything wrong?" Frau Schichtl asked sharply.
"Come, Paul, you don't have to pretend with me. Something *is* wrong." She turned to look at Lennox, and then
at the kitchen, as if her answer might be found there.
She noticed, for the first time, the dried mud on the sitting-room floor. She walked slowly toward it.

"Oh, Paul!" she said in dismay. "I scrubbed it only
yesterday afternoon." Then all her postponed emotion
broke. She began to cry.

"Now, Frieda," Mahlknecht was saying uncomfortably,
"we'll scrub it for you today. I'll tell you what happened
as soon as you are a sensible woman again. Perhaps this
rest from school will be good for you. You've been doing
too much."

"I have not." Frau Schichtl's tears were in control, but
her temper was ragged. It was the first time that Lennox
had seen her anything but calm and capable. Somehow
she was all the more human. "I have not. None of us
have. We've done too little. We let the Germans appoint
this and that. We do nothing but plan for the future.
What good is that to us now?"

"The Germans have the machine guns and we have
not," her brother said patiently. "We are a small collection of people. We are farmers. We have no factories,

no machines to help us. We can't make arms. We've stolen some from derailed trains, and from the Italians' barracks. But we haven't enough yet. If we use them now we'd be wiped out within a week. What good would we be then to the Allies or to ourselves? All we can do is to wait, to have our plans well made, to be ready. Then we can help in the fighting when the Allies are coming up towards the Brenner. There will be plenty of fighting and dying then, Frieda. But it will be useful fighting and useful dying. Ask Peter, here, if you don't believe me."

Frau Schichtl was silent. And then she said sadly, "I don't need to ask him. I just get so tired of waiting, that's all. And I get worried: he wants to leave. And Johann is seeing too much of that girl. He went to see her yesterday before he came home, and that's why he arrived only half an hour before you did, this dawn. He should have been here yesterday. And now this school business. The children will be questioned about their families, and their minds will be poisoned. They will be told the wrong things."

"What girl are you talking about?" Mahlknecht asked.

"Eva Mussner. Mussner's niece. She was in Bozen for the last five years, Johann saw her there. Now she's come back to Hinterwald. She opened up her uncle's house. She's staying there."

"Eva Mussner," Paul Mahlknecht said thoughtfully. "A skinny little thing with straight hair, I remember."

"She's hardly that now," Frau Schichtl answered tartly. "She met me in the village today. She was very upset about what happened. So she said."

There was a pause. Mahlknecht was lost in his thoughts.

"What was it you were going to tell me," Frau Schichtl asked at last, "about that mess of mud on my best sitting-room floor?"

"We had two visitors this morning. American flyers."

Frau Schichtl glanced at the ceiling. "They are sleeping now, I suppose."

"No. We sent them away." Mahlknecht began to light his pipe. "We don't think they were Americans, although they were dressed correctly. We think they are Germans."

"But, Paul, what if they aren't?" Frau Schichtl was roused once more. "How could you be so sure?"

"They said their plane had crashed many miles away, and that explained why they could arrive without us hearing their plane. But the houses are scattered so much over the Schlern that someone must have heard and seen the crash. And when flyers are dragged from their planes or are found wandering near them our rule is that someone accompanies them to the places where they can get a guide out of the mountains. They said a house had sheltered them near where they had crashed. But no one had been sent with them to prove to us that they had crashed. That made me wonder. The only men who would come as quietly and unannounced as they did would have been men who had parachuted on to the Schlern. That is what I thought they were when I went downstairs to meet them: but they didn't ask for Peter or for me, and they didn't give any of the right identifications. So I called Johann and Peter downstairs just to make sure that they were Americans. The slightest doubt, and we couldn't help them. Peter found a doubt." Mahlknecht began to laugh. He threw back his head as he had done when Lennox had first explained his trick, and his teeth were white against the dark beard. He was explaining it now, all over again. Frau Schichtl smiled too, and then a new worry appeared.

"If they were Germans, and you called Peter down here so that they could see him . . ." Frau Schichtl began. "Paul, how could you!"

"He didn't talk English, Frieda. In fact, he gave a good imitation of old Schroffenegger's style of conversation."

Lennox grinned self-consciously. He had often watched Josef Schroffenegger, one of the Committee men who came up to visit Frau Schichtl on Saturdays, with a good deal of amusement. Now that he considered it, he had given a sizeable imitation of the old warrior.

"What else could I have done, Frieda?" Mahlknecht went on. "I had to know if these men were real Americans. It was logical to believe that Peter would know more about judging them than we do. He has fought and lived beside them. And our risk did work. He did find out."

"Then they will blame him."

"No. I took care to do all the deciding. It is I whom they will blame. Anyway, all they can report is that we refused to help American flyers."

Lennox said, "Won't the Germans expect us to report these flyers?"

Mahlknecht smiled. "That is a good idea," he said. "But perhaps it is too good. The Germans might begin to wonder why we were suddenly so helpful. The only informers they have found are people like Mussner, and the Germans know them all. From the rest of us, they may not expect actual trouble, but they have learned this winter not to expect help either. They think we are a slow, pigheaded, selfish lot of peasants. They think we are inefficient and lazy. Unbiddable thickheads. No, we don't have to worry about reporting to the Germans. It would seem out of character." He smiled again, encouragingly, as he watched the younger man's face. "It was a good idea, well worth suggesting," Mahlknecht added. "We would have used it, if the Germans weren't so convinced that people fall into rigid classifications."

Frau Schichtl wasn't listening to this explanation. She was still worrying about two particular Germans. She asked impatiently, "So you sent Johann to warn the Committee? Do you think there will be more trouble?"

"We shall have to keep our eyes open. For if the Germans chose this house for their trick then they had some suspicion."

"Suspicion." the cold word set Frau Schichtl's face into a mask.

"Yes. Kasal's farm would have been a better place to find food or to hide. A farm has always more food than a cottage; it has outbuildings and barns. Yet they chose this house."

Frau Schichtl was silent. And then, looking at Lennox, she said, "What about Peter?"

Mahlknecht walked over to the window. "Roads are bad," he said, "but this part of the hillside always did trap most water. Can't judge by it. Most roads will be drying up by another week, and there are some parts of the woods that are passable even now. Schönau, for instance. I think Schroffenegger's lumber camp at Schönau will have to open early this spring. Schroffenegger has got his men all selected for it: we can trust each one of them. Peter will join them there. Ever cut down trees, Peter?"

Lennox shook his head.

"Good for you. Gives you exercise. Makes you fit."

They heard Johann's cheery whistle. He came in with high good humor. "Everything's all right," he said. "They must have been Germans. Didn't try any other houses. I saw all the local Committee, and they are keeping watch."

"You didn't see that Mussner girl, did you?" Frau Schichtl said.

Johann's smile faded. "What's she got to do with the two flyers?" he asked, defensively.

"Frieda, let me deal with this my way," Mahlknecht said, almost sharply. "Come on, Johann, lend us a hand with the scrubbing of this floor. You came just in time to help us clean it up. Your mother can start cooking dinner. We'll have it early, today. There's a lot of talking to be done tonight."

Frau Schichtl's hands went to her mouth. "I almost forgot," she said. "The Committee is coming up here this evening."

"And tomorrow at dawn there is the spring festival in

Hinterwald." Mahlknecht looked thoughtfully at his sister. "I wonder if the Germans timed their interest in our village just to coincide with our feast day. They know the people from miles around will be coming to Hinterwald tomorrow.

"Rubbish," Frau Schichtl said. "It is just the Germans being Germans. They always were too officious. They like making regulations and rules." She was trying on her large white apron over the small silk one which was part of her dress. She began to measure a meager quantity of flour into the large mixing bowl for the soup's dumplings.

"Not so much rubbish," Mahlknecht said quietly. "You don't like the Germans, Freida, but you don't know how they work. They've done things you couldn't believe just because you have lived among normal people most of your life. I am willing to wager that they chose our feast day for some reason. They know that everyone will be there. They will have us all gathered together like a flock of sheep."

"A feast day is a holy day," Frau Schichtl said. "Only heathens would cause trouble then." Her voice was indignant. Her hands kneaded the dough vigorously.

Mahlknecht shrugged his shoulders. "I can feel the screw going on," he said quietly. "That's all."

"I wonder just how much suspicion they have," Lennox said. "They may have discovered that there is active opposition here, even if it is hidden."

"Perhaps," admitted Mahlknecht. "And perhaps it is only the news which is worrying them."

"What news?" Lennox asked. For the last two nights it had been impossible to hear Allied broadcasts. There had been atmospherics and much interference. "What news?"

"The Brenner railway has been bombed. There has been a very thorough job. I left Bozen in flames two days ago. The German supply system has been wrecked. And the Allied push into Italy has begun."

Frau Schichtl stopped her work. She stared unbelievingly at her brother.

It's begun, Lennox kept thinking; at last it has begun. He said, "And no one has yet come here. The colonel didn't get through."

"On the contrary, he did. He sent some men to see me in Bozen. We have our plans all made, don't worry about that."

"And what about the men who were coming here?"

"They are coming. Any day now. Why the devil did you think I came to Hinterwald? Why the devil did I nearly break my neck this morning getting down those stairs?" Mahlknecht halted, looked at his sister and Lennox. "What's wrong with both of you?" he demanded. "Jumpy as a couple of cats. Filled with worries. Don't you trust me or our Allies? What do you think we are, anyway? A bunch of newly born lambs?"

Lennox smiled at that. "We've stopped worrying," he said. "If things have really started moving then we've stopped worrying. We'll have plenty to do instead."

Frau Schichtl was smiling too. "It's begun," she said happily. And then the smile vanished. She brushed some flour off her forearm. "I am glad. I am glad and I'm sorry. Sorry for the men who will die." She looked as if she were going to cry again. She began pummeling the small handfuls of dough as if they were Germans. "Why couldn't they leave everyone alone? Why couldn't they stay in their Germany? What's wrong with them?" Her voice was angry now. She slapped the dumplings into the pot of thin soup. "And I've probably ruined these. I've probably put in salt twice over." She suddenly hurried out of the kitchen and climbed the stairs to her room.

Mahlknecht ignored all this, although his face was grave as he gave Lennox his answer.

"Plenty to do," he said briefly, and turned to look out of the window at the green fields.

CHAPTER 12

Lennox woke to hear the first "Juch-hé!" coming down
the mountainside. Today, he remembered, was Hinterwald's feast day. He lay under the thin padded quilt, feeling the cold morning air strike round his ears. Again a
"Juch-hé!" sounded, and again. The last one was long-
drawn-out, with the accent on the *"Juch,"* while the last
syllable fell gradually away. The groups of men, women,
and children, making their way towards Hinterwald, were
silent once more. Now there was only the deep peace of
the darkness before dawn.

"Damned fools," he said, but he was smiling. He tried
it. There was something merry and high-spirited about the
yodeled call. It meant nothing except that the man who
called it, with his hands cupped round his lips, was feeling
in good form. "You're a damned fool too," he told himself.
And then he laughed. It was difficult this morning to work
up his usual awakening gloom.

But then, last night had been a good night. The Committee had met—the hatchet-faced old men, the serious grim-
eyed boys, talking of freedom. Freedom made good talk.
Last night it had been especially good. For the news from
Italy had wakened hope, and the winter plans were alive
at last. Lennox, sitting quietly back in his usual corner, had
watched with increasing interest the quickening faces
around him. He had seen them before, never all at
once but in various groups of two or three. Now the
eleven men (three from this district, the others from
more distant parts of the Schlern) had come together.

Openly, their reason was the feast of St. Johann, with its early mass in the morning, to which all the friends and relatives of the people of Hinterwald would come. Secretly, their purpose was a final meeting—with Paul Mahlknecht here from Bozen to give the latest report on anti-German organization—before the men scattered into the forests and onto mountain alps for the summer.

And Mahlknecht had brought encouraging news. Contact with the Allies had been made; the Committee's plans had been accepted. The band of prisoners from the camp above Bozen had fought their way through to the Allied lines, and Colonel Wayne, who had talked with Mahlknecht last September, was one of those who were still alive. His report had interested Allied Headquarters, and they had sent three men secretly to Bozen. There, in February, they had met Mahlknecht and some of his friends. They had listened and they had questioned. Then they had left Bozen, to make their way back to the Allies. In April one of them returned with fuller instructions. He was working in Bozen, now, along with the Committee of that district. Besides his instructions, he had brought the news that as soon as the snows melted on the high meadows two men would arrive on the Schlern. They were coming to help to prepare the way for still more Allies to come.

The Tyrolese listened with scarcely a flicker of emotion over their wind-tanned, hard-boned faces. Lennox knew them well enough now not to be deceived by such calm. His respect for them grew as he watched.

For one thing, he had gradually become more convinced during this long waiting winter of the worth of Mahlknecht's plans. At first he had been cynical; now he believed that they contained the germ of real help. For when the Allied armies drew near the difficult mountains of the South Tyrol—mountains which made South Italian peaks look like molehills—they would find people who were not only willing but ready to help. There was a list of men and women who could be completely trusted, a list of those who were neutral, a shorter but definite list of those who were enemies. They would find guides who could lead them over little-known mountain paths in infiltration movements and surprise attacks on German set positions. They would find women who would shelter the wounded; people who had measured their food supplies so that there would be enough; villages which could be responsible for order; men who would fight dependably and teach the tricks of the mountains. Practical help like that was something the Allied soldier could appreciate. When civilians didn't malinger or cheat, a soldier could get ahead with his job of fighting. That was all a soldier wanted.

For another thing, there was a broader possibility to Mahlknecht's plans. Last night Lennox had suddenly seen it. In his excitement he forgot all about his old dislike of responsibility. Perhaps the incident with the two pseudo-airmen had proved that there was a difference between taking responsibility and mere self-assertion. Anyway, he had risen to his feet and made a speech.

"These ideas are good," he had begun. "Why don't you spread them across the Brenner Pass into the North Tyrol? The people there are of your blood; they could be organized as you are organizing yourselves. They would listen to you. If our troops are to make quick progress they must find a population that is willing to help. They must find order, no politics being played, no nuisance refugees, and no mean profiteering at their expense. An army doesn't want volunteer recruits who haven't been trained in its way. Its striking power depends on being a single trained unit. But it does need people who will really help, and make themselves as little of a worry as possible. It needs people who will be dependable guides, people who will give accurate information, people who will use the supplies we send them to sabotage the right place at the right moment. If the North Tyrol will agree to that then you will have won us a battle. Remember that the North Tyrol borders Bavaria. And Bavaria is the back door into Germany.

That, Lennox decided as he lay under the quilt's warmth and watched the sky lighten into a cold gray, had been quite a speech. It had sort of overpowered him at the end. He had begun with a plea for wider help and had ended with the key to Germany's back door. It had sounded all right last night. And the Committee's reaction had been flattering: already the men, who could travel into the North Tyrol in small groups of two or three, were being chosen to make contact with anti-Nazi groups there. As Mahlknecht had said, plans north and south of the Brenner Pass could be co-ordinated: the Tyrol would be united once again. But, Lennox wondered as he watched the long streaks of yellow light split up the gray sky outside, did it sound so well this morning? For a man who had been in revolt against authority for so many years of his life, he had certainly gone off the deep end. The Committee's plans were already broadening to suit his idea: and on whose authority had he spoken? On his own. "By God," he said, suddenly subdued.

And then he wondered just for how many weeks the idea had been simmering in a secret place of his mind. Last night it had boiled over.

Again the call of *"Juch-hé!"* sounded. This time it was near. A group of people must be coming down past this house. He rose quickly and went to the window. Day had fully broken. The birds were wide awake and chattering. The pine forest was a mass of black-pointed shapes with golden highlights. The five lean cows were walking, in leisurely single file, out from the Kasal barn. The thin notes of the bells round their dun-colored necks jangled in broken rhythm. The Kasal family, dressed in their very best clothes, were standing stiffly at the doorway of their house. They were looking towards the pine forest, waiting for those who were walking into the village.

Then Lennox saw them too. Eight women and three men, five young boys and four girls. Today the men had given up their leather breeches and white wool stockings for tight black trousers tucked into high leather boots. The high white plumes on their slouched hats were held proudly. The women wore wide black skirts and bright aprons. They had thrown heavy shawls over their white silk blouses as a protection against the morning air. Their hats were broad-brimmed, with the tight, rounded crown cut flatly on top. Their hair was braided and twisted round their heads. Most of them were very fair. Lennox saw the gleam of pale gold under the black felt hats. They walked barefoot, with their white stockings and polished shoes carried carefully over the muddy paths. They would bathe their feet in some stream at the edge of the village, draw on their stockings and shoes, and then advance sedately towards the church. They would look as if they had just stepped out of their cottages instead of having walked for ten miles through the night.

One of the boys let out a yodel as he saw the waiting Kasals. From across the fields the *Juch-hé* call from another group. Higher up on the hillside there was a further burst of calls. It was the peasant way of contact and answer over mountain spaces. It was infectious. Even the birds had started to sing in a sudden frenzy of excitement. Lennox was tempted to lean out of the window, cup his hands round his mouth, and join in.

But there was a knock, and he turned away from the window to open his bedroom door. Frau Schichtl, along with her brother and son, entered in full regalia. Lennox, in his gray flannel nightshirt, swept them a low bow. "Most elegant," he said.

Frau Schichtl's face colored, and she looked pleased. She smoothed her red silk embroidered apron over the wide black skirt, adjusted the fringed scarf crossed over her breast, pulled the edge of her black lace mittens more closely to her elbow, straightened the strange-crowned hat. She smiled self-consciously. Then suddenly she laughed and said, "If only you could see yourself, Peter."

Lennox looked down at his bare calves, and was inclined
to agree. Then he looked at the elaborate costumes and
thought that remark could cut both ways. He smiled
blandly.

Johann said, "Pity you've got to stay here. After mass
and the procession the fun begins. Pity you couldn't come
down for the dance tonight." He spun his hat, with its soft
white feather, round on his hand. His gay clothes had
affected his spirits. His high boots beat out a brief sole and
heel rhythm. His face had lost the angry look it had kept
last night after his uncle had talked to him about the Mussner girl. He patted his black velvet waistcoat with its
pattern of red embroidered flowers, and pretended to polish
the silver buttons. "Not a bad fit, either," he admitted,
proudly surveying his father's clothes. "Well, we had better
start. Mass is at half past six. Time's shifting."

"You know where to find breakfast," Frau Schichtl said,
"I left the table ready for you last night. I wish you could
come." She looked at her brother.

Paul Mahlknecht shook his head. He had adopted a new
character with the traditional clothes: he was no longer the
man from Bozen. He was a man of the Tyrol, as quiet and
imperturbable as the mountains which brooded over the
meadows. In this costume he was keeping faith with his
father and grandfather and the fathers before them. This
was the symbol of his fight. This was the outward sign of
his inner loyalties. The man who wore these clothes so
confidently, so proudly, was a man who would never become either an Italian or a German.

Lennox was thankful he had resisted making that crack
about fancy dress which had almost rolled off the tip of
his tongue. He was now ashamed that he had even thought
about it. He glanced nervously at Mahlknecht's somber
face, and worried about mind reading.

But Mahlknecht was saying, "I'll return here before the
evening begins. We can talk together then." Frau Schichtl
and Johann were beginning to descend the stairs.

Lennox said quickly, " Do you think I could take a short walk this afternoon through the woods? Everyone will be down at the village. And if Germans watch this house— well, they already know that a disabled soldier lives here."

Mahlknecht nodded thoughtfully. He hadn't missed the urgency in Lennox's voice. "A walk would do you good," he said. "But don't go far away. I'd rather finish our talk. I shall have to leave here soon, you know."

"And what about the men you are expecting?"

"They should have arrived yesterday or the day before. Weather permitting, they should have arrived then."

"Parachuting in?"

Mahlknecht nodded. "I'll give you instructions tonight about identifying them, in case they come when I am away from the Schlern."

"It would be better if you were here to welcome them yourself."

"They will see me later. Besides they will want to talk to you." Mahlknecht grinned suddenly. "Just to make sure that your colonel and I haven't brought them here on a wild goose chase. You can tell them just what you think of us."

"I wonder why they didn't send someone before this," Lennox said, half angrily. "Devil of a way they've kept us hanging on."

"There was no need to have anyone here in the winter in addition to you," Mahlknecht reminded him. "They did a much cleverer thing. They sent men to talk to me in Bozen. That was all that was needed while winter lasted."

Yes, that's right: I was good enough as an outpost up here in the winter months when nothing happened, Lennox thought. But as soon as action starts and some real fun begins, then out goes the poor bloody infantry and in comes the professional officer.

Frau Schichtl's voice called from downstairs, "We are all waiting, Paul."

"Coming." Mahlknecht deceded the staircase. Halfway down he called softly, "You'll have your freedom soon, Peter. You can start your own plans again."

Then his light footsteps were crossing the sitting room, and the door closed softly. Lennox could imagine the smile on Mahlknecht's lips.

He closed his bedroom door, locking it automatically.

He deserved that last remark. He deserved the smile—if it had been there. He had wanted his freedom. He was getting it.

He walked back to the window. The group outside the Kasals' house had grown. They were waiting for Mahlknecht and his family. He watched the movement in the crowd—the white-plumed hats, the spreading black skirts, the tall men and women with their erect heads, the smooth golden hair of the laughing children. The older people walked first, the men leading the way. At the end of the procession he saw Johann. His hat was now jauntily set on his slicked hair. He was talking to Katharina Kasal, walking beside him with that long, effortless step which seemed natural to the women of this district. At the point in the winding road where it swerved behind a group of trees the Kasal girl halted. She turned and looked towards the Schichtl house. Then she went on.

Lennox drew back from the window. He had been leaning out, like a fool. He hadn't thought anyone would turn round to look this way. They were all so intent on their festival. He wondered if she had really seen him. What on earth had made her do that?

He peeled off the nightshirt and began the morning's usual stretch and bend. That was how he got exercise. Stretch and bend, and bend and stretch. Suddenly he remembered he was going to have real exercise today. Mahlknecht had given him the permission which Frau Schichtl had never been able to give. He could walk outside. He could taste free air. He wouldn't wait until this afternoon, either. He kicked the nightshirt aside, and poured the water out of the jug into the basin on his small bedroom table. The water held the night's cold air, but at least he hadn't to break the ice on it now before he could wash or shave.

He dressed quickly, remembering to take the gray woolen jacket which Frau Schichtl had found for him in her late husband's clothes' chest. It would be cold outside until the sun was really high. He ran downstairs, and stopped to pick up a slab of bread for his pocket. He opened the back door and looked at the high peaks with the sun rising up behind them. He took a deep breath of the cold, crisp air. It tasted differently down here. It couldn't be the same air which came into his room upstairs. It didn't seem the same air at all, with his feet free on this grass.

In the pine wood behind the house there was a narrow path hidden behind three tall trees clumped together. He had looked at it bitterly on every one of those rare nights in which he had walked to the edge of the wood. Now he stood hesitating, wondering if the path was still there, wondering if he had imagined it. He began walking slowly towards the three trees. He saw the beginning of the path. Suddenly, he started to run.

CHAPTER 13

Lennox explored the wood thoroughly. He found that its boundaries were very simple. On its west was the road which led past the Schichtl and Kasal houses. On its east was a steep hillside and, above that, the series of precipices which formed the mountain's peak. From the north edge of the wood he could see sloping meadow-land, a twisting road, scattered houses, distant villages gathered round church spires, and a sea of mountains as background to all this. From the south edge, there was the road curving down to Hinterwald. But the village itself was hidden by trees. Only the church, with its onion-shaped spire, and a few chalets were to be seen. Beyond the trees of Hinterwald were falling and rising fields, and then more mountains. There were mountains everywhere.

On these four sides of the wood Lennox had rested and stared at the views. They were incredible. He had often admired rows of savage mountains, but in this country they were strangely combined with smiling meadows and wide stretches of wooded slopes. The scattered chalets, the small neat villages, gave a comforting feeling. Mountains alone dominated and threatened. But here, pleasant houses and a picturesque church and a comfortable inn would welcome you at the end of a lonely walk. This would be a country worth exploring. A man could find peace here.

Now it was almost midday, and he ate his piece of bread, and slowly drank a mouthful of water from a clear icy stream. He settled himself on a rock sheltered by the last fringe of trees on the high east side of this wood. The wood covered a steep incline from the mountain's stony base to the Schichtl house, so that he could sit here and watch the pines drop away in front of him and look at the far mountains to the west. Over there was the Brenner railway in its deep valley, and beyond it the western mountains, and beyond them the Swiss Alps. He thought, at this moment I don't believe I have ever been happier in my life. He remembered suddenly that he should be amazed, and yet he wasn't. He looked at his scarred right hand. "Get well, blast you," he said. "You've got to paint. Now you've found something to paint." He was grinning like an idiot. "You're drunk," he told himself. "Drunk with this feeling of being free. Drunk with all this peace and beauty. You're drunk."

Certainly, he felt wonderful. Those two Germans neatly handled yesterday, the successful meeting last night. Mahlknecht's plans no longer hopeless but fitting nicely into the latest news from the Allied front in Italy—all these contribued to this sense of jubilation. And he could laugh at himself again. This view of mountains and unlimited space put everything into proper perspective.

He rose, somewhat stiffly, carrying his jacket jauntily over one shoulder, and began the descent to the house. He was hungry, and thought with pleasure of the remains of some cold meat in the larder. He would reheat some of Frau Schichtl's excellent soup. There was rich milk from the Kasal farm, and white bread baked only yesterday. He remembered the sour, stale food of the prison camps, and the meal he was going to prepare seemed an epicure's delight. Then, after a leisurely dinner with some of the German-published newspapers, which Mahlknecht had brought from Bozen, to provide amusement on the side, He would—He halted his thoughts with his stride. He stopped close to a tree. Standing quite still, he listened intently. He heard nothing. Yet he sensed movement. Someone was coming quietly towards him. He drew quickly behind the tree, and prayed that its cover was adequate.

Then he saw the wide-skirted black dress and its bright silk apron. Above the gay scarf, with its tapering ends crossed demurely over her breast, was the face of the Kasal girl. She was looking puzzled, as if she had heard him and was now wondering where he had gone. She hesitated, and then stopped. There was something so pathetic in her sudden dejection, in her hesitation as her eyes anxiously searched the path ahead of her, that Lennox stepped forward into the open. She flinched at that, and her hand went quickly to her heart. But she didn't cry out. And then she was smiling, and all the worry was gone from her eyes. They were very blue. Her hair, so smoothly parted and brushed back from the high forehead and with its long, thick plaits circling her head, was very fair. The color in her checks had been deepened by her haste. She came forward to where he stood, walking with that easy step of hers. She was broadshouldered and tall, taller than he had imagined, and her body was well-shaped and strong. Good bones, he observed with a professional eye, and a face molded in excellent proportions. It was a calm face, and a strong face, and a face still so filled with hope and belief that Lennox felt sorry for her. She wouldn't look so trusting as that in ten years' time. She'd learn that the world wasn't so big and beautiful by then.

She said in her quiet voice, "Uncle Paul sent me." He stopped thinking about the girl. He was suddenly alert.

"Yes?" he asked.

"He will not be back here tonight. Two friends have arrived."

Peter Lennox watched her face: it was evident that she knew the message was important, but he was equally sure she didn't know the reason of its importance.

"Where is Johann?" he asked.

"He's with Uncle Paul. They want you to bring them their everyday clothes. You'll find them on the chairs in their room. Bundle them up tightly—everything you see there. I'll go to our house and change my dress. I can't travel quickly in this." She looked down at the silk apron, at the silver buttons on the black silk bodice, at the wide skirt banded at the hem with embroidery. She was smiling at the very idea. She suddenly noticed the look, half puzzled, half anxious on Lennox's face. "I shall lead you to Johann and Uncle Paul," she said. "They are only about three miles away from here. But they are a difficult three miles."

"What's happened?" Just when all the plans seemed ripe something had gone wrong. His good temper had vanished: he was worrying and heartsick once more.

"Nothing. Not yet. Some Germans have come to the village. They've opened a police station, and they've put up notices that all men must register there today. The Germans are watching the processions and the people. They are very quiet and friendly. But they have two trucks hidden half a mile from the village. Andreas Wenter saw them as he was taking a short cut to the village this morning. Paul Mahlknecht thinks the trucks have come for men to work in labor gangs on the Brenner railway. That's what some of us think, although many won't believe it. But the younger men believe it. They've listened to Paul Mahlknecht. They are all slipping out of the village before the dance begins this evening, for that's when the Germans would expect all the young people to be together."

She had already started to descend the path. He caught up with her, his mind still filled with questions.

"Why were *you* sent here?" he asked.

She answered, "I was sent home by my mother. I'm in disgrace." She wasn't smiling. She was very serious, and he restrained a laugh in time.

"What . . . ?" he began. But she shook her head. "Later," she said. "We must hurry now."

He was thinking partly that she was neither so young nor so helpless as he had first thought; and partly that the people of Hinterwald must be having a difficult time at their feast-day celebrations. What with Germans . . . two important strangers wandering in to join the fun . . . mothers sending daughters home in disgrace. . . . He wondered if the stolid faces were still as expressionless, if the processions and all the other formalities were still following the usual routine. The postponed laugh began to take shape, and couldn't be controlled this time.

"It isn't funny," the girl said reproachfully.

"No," he agreed, "it isn't funny." But he went on laughing to himself.

The sound of a motorcar checked him. The girl looked at him anxiously. They halted, listening, judging the distance by sound. The car stopped. It was near them; perhaps in front of the Schichtl house. Quickly, he grasped her arm and led her to the left. They must get off this path. The girl not only understood that, she was untying the too-bright apron from her waist, folding it up tightly to carry in her hand. If Lennox hadn't been so worried he would have been surprised. She understood, all right.

"Let's get to the edge of the wood. Let's see," he whispered. She nodded, following him obediently. He must see, he thought desperately. He had to know what was happening down on that road.

When they reached the edge of the wood it was the girl who led him to a point where the trees were thick enough for safety. From there they could watch the Schichtl house and the Kasal farm and the road in between. Lennox nodded, well-pleased.

He could see the car, drawn up at the left corner of the Schichtl house. German, of course. None of the people of this district owned a car. Two men were seated in the car, waiting. Civilian dress. Two others in black uniform were coming out of the Schichtl house. They halted at the car. Much talking. The two civilians got out of the car. The two uniforms got in. The car, slipping in the mud, was turned around and pointed back to the village. The two civilians walked towards the Kasal farm. They went into the house. Then came out. Then they walked round to the barn at its side. One was offering the other a cigarette. They were settling down for a long watch. They were hidden now by the barn. They didn't reappear.

Lennox drew a deep breath. The girl was saying, her voice desolate, worry drawing her brows together, "We must leave now. Without food or proper clothes. We must leave."

Lennox was thinking. So they *were* Germans. We were right. They were Germans, and not American flyers. For the two civilians, who had so leisurely lighted cigarettes and had wandered so innocently towards the cover of the farm buildings, were of the same build and size and coloring as the two men who had come yesterday to the Schichtl house. Somehow he was suddenly glad of this moment which had proved yesterday's decision.

"Please." The girl was shaking his arm. "Please, we must go. We must get to Schönau and tell them. We must go." She was frightened now.

Lennox touched her shoulder encouragingly. "Don't worry," he said awkwardly. "They've only chosen your barn so that they can have a comfortable front view of the Schichtl house."

She nodded, and bit her lip. "We must tell Uncle Paul," she said. "Come." He realized then that she wasn't afraid for the Kasal house: her fear was for the Schichtls. They backed carefully away from the outside fringe of pines. and then, safely in the depth of the wood, they began to climb. Lennox didn't speak at first. He was trying to get his thoughts into order. These two Germans had come back to the Schichtl house because they could identify the men in it. But why had they come back? Why the openly official visit? Had they learned his true identity? They were waiting, certainly. For what? For him, or for Paul Mahlknecht, or for . . . He suddenly thought of the two "friends" whom the girl had mentioned in her first sentence. Had they been seen landing, and followed? Had their parachutes been discovered? Was the Schichtl house naturally suspected?

Was the search on? He suddenly felt that he knew only half of this danger: Mahlknecht and Johann would know the other half. Together, they'd form a clearer picture. He forgot he was tired, forgot he was hungry. He only remembered the need to get to this Schönau, wherever it was. He followed the girl, watching the way she moved so easily, so capably. Mahlknecht had been right: the people who lived in this country made excellent guides. They knew the terrain: walking and climbing was a natural way for them to spend their free time. It was as natural for them to scale these mountains above, as it was for people at home to put on their best hats on Sunday afternoons for a stroll in the parks. He kept the girl's steady pace, content to let her choose the path.

CHAPTER 14

They had come to the northeast corner of the wood. The lower mountain slope, with its mixture of grass and boulders and small shrubs, lay before them.

The girl spoke for the first time. "We cross this until we reach the valley, which leads up in between that group of mountains." She pointed to three towering peaks of rock. "Schönau is the name we give the alp in the middle of the high forest up there."

Lennox nodded. He could neither see any valley, nor any sign of a higher forest. All he could see were the bold precipices of the mountains and this lower slope falling to the wood where they now stood.

"Where's the path?" he asked.

"Here." She smiled. "You will get accustomed to seeing it. It is difficult for strangers' eyes at first."

Lennox said nothing. He still couldn't see any path. She sensed his annoyance, for she turned the conversation politely. "You knew where I lived. Do you know my name too?"

"Katharina Kasal."

She laughed and said, "And I know who you are."

He pretended to smile. He said very quietly, "And who am I?"

"Peter Schichtl, of course."

His smile became easier. "How did you know I was Peter Schichtl?"

She hesitated, looking sideways at him, and then said with considerable embarrassment, "I saw you. I saw you sometimes taking a short walk to the wood at night. My bedroom window has a good view of this wood, you see. Then one day I asked your aunt who you were."

"And what did your father and mother say?" He tried to keep his voice amused, but he wasn't feeling quite so casual as his question. Alois Kasal was one of the men on Mahlknecht's doubtful list: Alois Kasal was a most annoying neutral. Suddenly the whole winter of secrecy and imprisonment seemed a complete farce.

The girl's quiet voice said, "I didn't tell my father or my mother. I was supposed to be asleep, not standing at a window looking at night on the mountains. You see," and she was smiling, "I am always doing wrong things."

"What did you do that was wrong today?"

She looked at him, and she was suddenly grave. "You shouldn't keep laughing at me," she said with Frau Schichtl-like dignity. "It was nothing very much, anyway. I gathered the school children and told them not to go back to school until Frau Schichtl was again their teacher."

"You did what?" His voice was suddenly serious. "Who heard you?"

"The children. And then my mother and Eva Mussner arrived just as I was finishing my talk."

He looked at her so intently that she lost her smile. "You are just as bad as my mother or Eva Mussner," she said angrily. "Don't you see something has got to be done about the school? Now, hurry; I have got to take you to Schönau and then get back home before my mother or father returns. Don't you understand?"

"I didn't." He was abrupt and angry. He wasn't thinking about the need for hurry. He was still thinking about this girl's words in the village. And Eva Mussner had heard them. "I am only asking you questions to try to understand. You don't explain much, do you?"

She didn't answer, but turned her back to him. She was taking off her stockings and shoes. She faced him once more, her cheeks still more highly colored. "My mother would be angrier if I were to ruin these shoes," she said. She laid the shoes and stockings and the pink apron neatly together behind a large rock, placing a stone carefully over them as an anchor.

"It won't be comfortable walking that way," he said.

She shrugged her shoulders. "I've no choice. Now we'll hurry."

"May we talk? I'd like to hear what has been happening at the village." He had started worrying again. The name of Eva Mussner was a bad omen. He began to wonder how much she had actually learned from Johann. The boy had sworn last night that he had told her nothing, but some women didn't need to be told very much. They guessed too easily. And now she had heard Katharina inciting a revolt among the school children. He didn't like this Eva Mussner. He didn't like her at all.

Katharina said, "Of course we can talk—if we have any breath left. But I've already told you all about today in the village." She started forward impatiently. She obviously thought that this Schichtl nephew wasn't very bright. And Lennox didn't argue. As a Tyrolese, he ought to have had a picture of today in the village quite clearly fixed in his mind's eye. He followed her in silence, noting that there was indeed a path, barely perceptible and narrow as a sheep track. It led them north, away from Hinterwald. Gradually it ascended the steep shoulder of the hillside. Above them, to the right, were the large teethlike ridges of dolomite rock. The sun was warm now. There was silence everywhere. There was no other living thing in sight.

When the roughest piece of climbing was over Lennox said determinedly, "Tell me everything that happened from the moment you left your house this morning."

Katharina threw a quick glance over her shoulder. Her face showed surprise, but her pace kept the same unbroken rhythm.

"Is it important?" she asked. "Really important?"

"Yes." He had to know. It might tell him why the Germans had come back to the Schichtl house. He had to know whether they were there to question, or there to arrest. He knew, when she began to talk, that she was trying to obey him fully. For she began with the moment when she had looked back at the Schichtl house. Sometimes she would pause and say, "Am I telling you too many things? Do you want all this?" And he would answer, "Go on. This is what I want to know." He began to feel as if he had been in Hinterwald himself that day. He became more sure of his judgment.

First there had been mass at the little church. Then there had been a procession. The holy image of St. Johann was carried through the village balanced on the shoulders of four young men. Behind them walked the older men, then the women, then the children. Late-comers in everyday clothes waited quietly at the side of the street. This year a larger crowd than ever had gathered to watch the festival. Many had come from distant villages. Some had come from other districts and valleys. It was a true gathering-day.

Among those dressed in ordinary peasant clothes were two men whom Katharina couldn't remember. But they must have been relatives or friends of Josef Schroffenegger, for they sat at his breakfast table in the Hotel Post's garden after the procession. Josef Schroffenegger had a large party around him that morning. There were two men from the Grödner-Tal and one from Seis, and one from the Tschamin-Tal. Paul Mahlknecht and other men of the Hinterwald had talked to the two strangers, too. So, although Katharina couldn't remember who they were, they were certainly recognized by Paul Mahlknecht and Josef Schroffenegger and their friends. Eva Mussner had asked who they were, and the owner of the Hotel Post had said, "Don't you remember them? Why, they are Ludwig Plank's boys, who used to live over in the Grödner-Tal." And then of course everyone remembered Ludwig Plank, and no one had asked anything more about his sons. Eva

Mussner said of course they had changed, and Frau Schichtl had said, "Well, none of us get any younger."

After breakfast there was a second procession—this time with a band and gay music. It was then that the Germans appeared. They were dressed in police uniforms. They stood outside the Golden Roof Inn, and they were enjoying the music. But all round the village large notices had been posted while the people had eaten breakfast. The notices said that every man between the age of eighteen and fifty-five years was to register at the new police station today. No one paid much attention to all this, because no one was going to bother to register. They hadn't registered last February when that regulation had been made a law. They weren't going to register now. Six German policemen weren't going to make them. Then the man Wenter arrived.

He was very late. His wife had just given birth to twins, and he had hurried from his farm to tell the good news to his friends in Hinterwald. He came by shortcuts over little-used paths. That was how he had seen the two German trucks, and German soldiers sitting on the grass beside them. The trucks were well-hidden, and they were scarcely a mile from the village. Wenter didn't let the Germans see him. He came to Hinterwald and told everyone about the twins. Then he had joined the procession, walking between Schroffenegger and Plank's sons. Before the time for resting came, when the women went visiting in the different houses and the men gathered round the tables in the inns, everyone who could be trusted knew about the German trucks. Only people like Mussner hadn't been told; everyone was avoiding them, anyway.

It was then that Katharina had gathered the older village children together and had told them to stay away from school. It was then that her mother had found her, and sent her home at once. People spoke to her as she left the village: no one knew why she was leaving, for her mother would tell no one the real reason. And among those who had spoken to her was Paul Mahlknecht. He gave her the

message for the Schichtl house. If she didn't find Peter
Schichtl at home she would find him walking in the wood.
She must go quietly, she must not call to him, she must wait
at the path until she saw him. She had done what she had
been told.

The girl's voice, as regular as her step, now halted. Then,
when he didn't speak, she said, "Now have I told you
enough?"

"Yes." He was still seeing, in his mind's eye, the crowd
of gaily dressed farmers and foresters with their quiet wives
and handsome daughters. He saw Schroffenegger's two
strange "friends," merging into this natural background.
After what he had been told he felt that the Germans were
merely there to press-gang the stronger men for the army
or for labor camps. The two strangers would never have
been allowed to walk in the procession if the search had
been for them: they would have been arrested in the first
five minutes. And, as he thought still more about it, he felt
that the Germans who had visited the Schichtl house today
and the Germans who had watched the procession in the
village had different purposes. The latter had wanted labor-
ers. The former—well, that was something he still had to
find out.

The girl said, "But you are still puzzled. What else can
I tell you?"

"Nothing." He was surprised at the gentleness of his own
voice. Its bitter edge had gone. "You've told me everything.
That's what I wanted to hear."

They halted now that they had reached a spur of sloping
rock. In the shelter of a large boulder they rested. The
wood, and the road to Hinterwald past the Schichtl house,
was far below them.

The girl watched him curiously as he looked at the long
stretch of country sloping away from him. So much peace,
he was thinking, and yet so much threat of danger. Peace
and yet no peace.

"Whom do you hate most?" he asked suddenly.

She stared at him in surprise. "Once I would have said the Italians. Now I say anyone who comes into my country and says that it is his. I hate him, whoever he is."

"Someone once said, 'Let them hate, provided that they fear.' "

She frowned as she followed the meaning of his words. And then she smiled. "But what if we don't fear?"

He smiled too. "There is no answer to that," he said, with a good deal of feeling. He gripped both of her shoulders, and held them tightly. They stood there smiling—as Lennox suddenly thought—like a couple of imbeciles. His hands dropped to his side.

"Where's this valley of yours?" he asked quickly. "I don't believe it exists."

"But it does!" She took his hand, and walked beside him, pulling him gently on. "Look! There it is." She was watching him again, not curiously this time. Whatever he had said in these last minutes had been the right thing to say. It wasn't mere politeness now which kept her smiling. She liked him, without knowing why he was here and with no conditions attached. He kept smiling too: somehow he felt like a human being again.

CHAPTER 15

The narrow valley, a gorge of rushing water deep down in the cleft of mountains, led them eastward. Lennox, looking upward at the jagged peaks above him on either side, felt as if he were buried in mountains. Ahead of him were mountains too, crest rising behind crest towards the eastern Alps. He was climbing with considerable effort along the narrow path which followed the turbulent rush of water, digging in with his feet, holding on with his hands. Katharina seemed as confident as the pine trees which grew so boldly on the steep banks. He had long since given up admiring the beauties of nature, and concentrated on following the girl.

Even when the path ended abruptly she didn't pause, but led him towards the source of the stream—a series of waterfalls cascading down the ledges of the mountain precipice. He stared at the lowest fall, where the arc of whitened water plunged into a turbulent pool before it raced down through the gorge. We are stuck, completely stymied, he thought; she's made a mistake—we have taken the wrong path. And his annoyance at having been outwalked and outclimbed vanished, and he felt sorry for the girl. She had tried so hard to help.

"Too bad," he said commiseratingly, but the noise of the falling water blotted out his words. Katharina smiled, said something which he couldn't hear either, and then laughed. He laughed too, just to cheer her up. Inwardly he was groaning at the idea of having to retrace his steps over that path. She had said Schönau was three miles from the

Schichtl house. They must have traveled well over two miles. If they had found the right path they would have almost been at Schönau by this time. Inwardly he began cursing.

The girl was pointing to his shoes. He got the idea that she was telling him to remove them. At her instruction, he rolled up his white footless half-stockings almost to reach his leather breeches. "Legs wash and dry more quickly than wool," she shouted, and then laughed once more at the whisper of her words. She picked up her wide skirt and innumerable layers of starched petticoats, drawing them up to her knees. Lennox noted the shape of her legs with approval. And then he was jolted out of his admiration as she stepped onto the soft ground where the path ended, and he realized he was supposed to follow her. Her precautions were justified. By the time they reached the waterfall and were walking over rocks, smoothed by floods and weather, their legs were generously coated with the rich black earth which comes from centuries of dying trees. As the fine spray of falling water pinpricked his brow, Lennox looked at the girl in amusement.

"Do we just walk through it?" he shouted, and decided that sarcasm needed a quiet voice.

But she nodded seriously. She pointed, and he saw a rocky ledge which ran out from the bank to disappear under the waterfall.

He shook his head. "Not I," he said decidedly.

She laughed at that, and placing her mouth against his ear, said, "The water falls out from the mountain, not down it. There's a shallow cave hidden behind that sheet of water. Four men could walk abreast under the fall. Come."

She didn't wait for him to finish his headshaking. She started over the rocky bank of the torrent, along the ledge. She seemed to disappear into the fine spray. He was left alone on the bank, staring at the boiling pool. He cursed, and then called her name. There was only the roar of

water for an answer. He cursed again and began to walk
slowly over the ledge. The foothold was slippery, and the
rock against which his hand balanced was too wet for any
secure grasp. But strangely, the spray was less strong here
than it had been on the bank. Soon it had ceased, and the
ledge had broadened. It was as the girl had said. A shallow
cave had been hollowed out of the mountain face, a place
of cold shadow. The sun's rays were broken and trapped
by a curtain of water. There was only a strange green light
and a constant dull roar, like the continuous grinding of
heavy wheels on cobbled stones. The world outside didn't
exist.

He stood and stared at the sheet of water which fell in
front of him. Now he began to see the texture of the torrent, like long close strands of gleaming silk. But the noise
blotted out even his thoughts: he felt he couldn't even hear
himself think. He felt the broadened ledge, watching it
narrow, feeling the spray sprinkle his face and hands and
legs once more. And then he was out into a world of
blinding yellow light, and he was groping carefully along
the narrow foothold with his hand once more balancing
him. The waterfall was behind him. The girl was waiting
on the other bank. She had washed the mud from her legs
and feet, and she was now carefully shaking down her
skirt and petticoats.

"You can put on your shoes again," she advised. "We
travel a short distance through pine trees now. No mud to
worry about there."

He washed the mud away beside a small inlet of water
at the bank, and drew on his shoes. He was still staring at
the waterfall. And it still didn't look possible. He felt a
fool, but anyway he had been a logical fool. It didn't look
possible that anyone could walk under that sheet of water.
From the bank, the ledge looked only a natural roughness
in the face of rock.

The girl was examining a smear of green on the wide
sleeve of her blouse. "That rock!" she said in disgust. "It's

oozing slime. Now I *must* get home before my mother does, so that I can clean this." She began to hurry up through the pine wood which covered this part of the mountainside. Lennox chased after her. His legs were tiring now. He kept pace with her only with difficulty. He didn't talk, but the girl pretended not to notice.

"The lumber camp is just five minutes away now," she said. "There's a broad meadow up there. That's Schönau."

When he still didn't say anything she went on cheerfully, "The real road to Schönau lies along the north side of the valley. That's the way the foresters and their carts come. But this short cut along the south side is very useful. We keep a watch on the north road, and if we don't like who is coming then we take the south shortcut back to the village. Johann once spent two hours in that cave under the waterfall while the Italians searched all around for him."

He nodded. He was saying to himself, "You damned superior fool to get angry because a girl had more sense than you had; because a girl can walk this way on bare feet and you've got to have shoes; because she's as fresh as a daisy and you're dead beat." And, having admitted his damned superior foolery, he was able to smile. The girl seemed to have understood, for she was smiling too. She pointed to the liberal green smears on his clothes, evidence that he had hugged the wall of the waterfall too closely. They both began to laugh.

Johann was standing behind a tree at the edge of the wood, watching this path so quietly that they hadn't noticed him.

"Thought you were never coming," he grumbled. He looked at them accusingly. "That path is supposed to be a shortcut, you know. Come on. All the rest of us are here." He gave a short whistle as a warning signal to the others wherever they were.

"I had to walk in my best dress," Kathraina explained. "We came as quickly as we could." It was a neat feminine

excuse, all the neater because she didn't look at Lennox
to place the blame on him.

Lennox didn't have to speak, because Johann had
grasped his arm and was walking beside him, talking in
that hoarse, confidential whisper of his. "One's an American. One's English. Both were dropped by parachute about
six miles from here. They went to Schroffenegger's house.
He brought them to us. They are all right. We are sure of
them. They knew all the right questions and answers."

The wood thinned. At its edge there was a forester's
hut. Before them was a broad stretch of fine green grass
with isolated trees. A cart track wound down into the valley. That would be the usual road, which followed the
valley back to Hinterwald as Katharina had described. The
hut door was open, and Paul Mahlknecht was standing in
its shadow. He looked pleased. At least, he was grinning
widely. He put his arm round Lennox's shoulders and drew
him into the hut.

"Your friends are here," he said.

Lennox looked over his shoulder, out at the green grass
and the sunlight and the twisted oak trees. Johann was
there, but Katharina had gone.

"Don't worry. We've two men out there watching the
north road," Mahlknecht said, misinterpreting that look.
"We are well protected."

"Where's the girl?" Lennox asked quickly.

"What? Missing her already?" said Mahlknecht, with
mock concern, and he began to laugh. His head was thrown
back, his teeth were white against the dark, bearded face.
Johann and old Schroffenegger were laughing too. The two
strangers smiled politely and looked at each other, as if the
joke might be funny but not quite so funny as all that.

Lennox said angrily, "She shouldn't have gone back to
her house. There are two Germans in her father's barn
now."

The laughter ceased. Lennox explained quickly. The
faces round him became more serious. He ended with

the true reason why Katharina had been sent home from the village by her mother. The faces were thoughtful now.

"She went back just after I met them," Johann explained worriedly to his uncle. Then, as if to convince himself, "She'll be all right. Katharina will follow the wood almost to Hinterwald before coming down into the road. She won't walk straight out of the wood at our house. The Germans will only think she is coming back from the village."

"That is, if that Mussner girl doesn't tell them when Katharina was sent home from the village," Lennox said. "Or why," he added grimly.

Johann moved to the door. "I'll see if I can catch up with Katharina. What shall I do? Give her warning, or bring her back here? If she doesn't return home her mother will have a search party out for her. The whole village will be talking then."

Mahlknecht glanced worriedly at the two polite strangers. He had a habit of biting the corner of his lip when he was working out a problem. He must have solved it, for his lower lip suddenly covered his top one determinedly, and his chin was more aggressive than ever.

He said, "She can't come here, obviously. Tell her to go to her aunt's house and stay there today. Her aunt can let her mother know where she is."

Johann nodded. He saluted them all with a perky forefinger, and stepped outside.

Lennox moved quickly to the door. "She will have to pass the large boulder at the northeast corner of our wood. She left her shoes and apron there."

"Bet you I find her before she leaves the torrent," Johann said, and with a parting grin which split up his face into two wide curves, he began a steady, loping run. There was something very neat and compact and capable about his movements.

Lennox was thinking of the boy's cool confidence. It wasn't boasting. Johann would probably overtake Katharina before she had traveled very far. He began to share the boy's quiet assurance, and he realized that if ever anything were to come of Mahlknecht's plans then he and these two other strangers would have to learn to trust the people of the mountains. For they knew their own capabilities, and they didn't claim anything beyond what they could do. He remembered the incident at the waterfall: certainly he had been too quickly discouraged there. And as he turned to enter the foresters' hut and meet the men who had arrived on the Schlern Lennox was thinking that perhaps nothing was so difficult, or so easy, as it first seemed.

CHAPTER 16

"Come and meet your friends," Mahlknecht was saying. Lennox came into the room slowly, his tired muscles jibing at him.

It was a simple place, divided for sleeping and for eating. One half of the room had a wooden table and benches, shelves—obviously for dishes—and a cupboard—probably for food. The other half had a row of rough wooden bunks along its walls. In the center of the wall opposite the door was a crude stone fireplace. The four windows were high-placed, small, and sheltered by the deep, jutting roof. They gave a feeling of snugness and security to the room.

The two strangers rose from the table. He suddenly realized that they were as wary of him as he was of them. They had given the right questions and answers; that was what Johann had said. But he still looked them over, as carefully as they were watching him. Leather trousers, embroidered braces, rough gray jackets not too new, collarless white shirts opened at the neck, battered felt hats with a jaunty feather, white stockings, heavy climbing boots with coarse leather laces. Their faces were tanned with sun and reddened by wind. Both were fair-haired, both were thin and yet tough-looking. One had snub features and gray eyes. The other had sharper features and blue eyes. Both sets of eyes were equally watchful. Both men could have been anything, pure Tyrolese for that matter. He couldn't even guess which was American, which was English. Their anonymity was striking: they had the kind

of face which you forget easily and remember with diffi
culty.

Old Schroffenegger nodded approvingly. "Well, you'l
all know each other again." He laughed. "They are al
good Tyroler. Look, Paul: they don't move a muscle. Goo
Tyroler. Why, I remember when the Italians used to mee
each other there would be embracing and kissing. They di
more kissing than our women." His thin hands slappe
the two nearest shoulders with surprising strength. "W
can work with these dour faces, can't we, Paul! Eh?"

The two strangers and Lennox weakened enough t
exchange a self-conscious grin. Their tension relaxed.

"Can't imagine us wasting kisses on each other," th
blue-eyed man said. He spoke in English, and judging from
his voice, he was an Englishman.

The gray-eyed man's smile broadened. "No darne
fear." He turned back to the bench and sat down. "W
were just making sure, that was all. You fit the colonel'
description all right."

Lennox said, "But I have still to make sure. The colone
couldn't give me any description of you."

The Englishman looked at him appraisingly.

"Fair enough," he said at last. "Well, I am Roy Shaw
captain, Royal Sussex Regiment. This is William Thomson
captain, Signal Corps, United States Army. We were bot
sent here to follow up information given by Colonel Wayn
after his escape from a prisoner-of-war camp outside o
Bozen. Shall I have to go on describing the colonel's gray
ing hair; or the wound on Private John Stewart's forehea
and the dyed coat he was wearing—your coat once,
believe; or Corporal William Ferry's views about the mos
hated guard at the prison camp whose name was Falcone?"

So Jock and Bill Ferry had got through. . . . "Goo
old—" he began, and then halted. He felt a fool: he, th
amateur, had challenged the professionals in what mus
have seemed a very naïve way. He gave Shaw a grudgin
good mark for his patience. He also remembered the wor

captain. He drew himself erect. "No sir," he said. His face was too expressionless.

"Cut that out," Thomson said, grinning.

Shaw nodded his agreement. "We won't get very far, that way," he said. He sat down at the table. "Come on, Lennox, take a seat and tell us how you've been holding the fort. How did the winter go? How serious are these chaps?" He looked at Mahlknecht and Schroffenegger. "That's the first thing we want to know."

Mahlknecht had probably not understood the quickly spoken words, but he had interpreted Shaw's look correctly enough.

"We'll leave you here and take a walk down to the woods to watch the south path for Johann," he suggested. He walked to the door. "One of us may have to go down later to the Kasal barn just to make sure there is no trouble." That was all he said, but Peter Lennox knew he was worried too.

The three foreigners watched the two men walk into the sunlight with their solid, heavy tread.

"It's tough on them," Thomson said. "Underground resistance is the toughest fight of all. It's the women that make it so tough. That girl you were worrying about, for instance. . . ."

"It's easier for us," Shaw agreed. "Our wives and children are safe at home. But here, a German can use them as blackmail." He looked at Lennox thoughtfully. "Do the men up here know what they are letting themselves in for?"

Lennox nodded. "We've talked about it this winter. They know that there can be no successful resistance unless the women are with them. If a wife starts weeping she'll hold her husband back. That's what old Schroffenegger said. But as far as I could make out, the women here do not go in for much weeping. They'll follow their men, and they'll take the risks."

His voice was grim, and he eyed the other two bitterly.

Shaw noticed that look. "I know," he said quietly, "our arrival spells trouble for many people. And yet if we hadn't been asked to come here then there would have been no spirit of resistance, no proof that these people weren't collaborationists. There's no easy way for an occupied country. They fight either on our side or on the other. Inaction and neutral thoughts fight for the other side. That's how you have to measure it. You count the facts and avoid imagination. That's what you've got to do."

His words made sense. But, Lennox thought, Shaw hadn't lived with those people for eight months. They were part of a military plan to these two men: they weren't Frau Schichtl and Johann and Katharina Kasal and old Schroffenegger. He said nothing. He watched the calm face and the cold eyes. The American, too, had lost his bitter emotion. He was equally matter-of-fact and objective.

Shaw's colorless voice went on, "We'll get down to the business on hand. Lennox, you've said the people here will accept the consequences. Do you mean they have all agreed to act?"

Lennox hesitated. It would have sounded better if he could have answered yes; but that wouldn't have been accurate. "Many of them have agreed. All those whom Mahlknecht can trust."

The American said, "Our information is that in the plebiscite of 1939 the Austrians of the South Tyrol were sharply divided. Some hundred and eighty-five thousand voted to leave the South Tyrol to go to Austria. Up to date only about seventy per cent have been transshipped. The other eighty-two thousand voted to stay here and become Italian citizens. From your observations here this winter, can you add anything to these facts?"

Lennox said, "Statistics in this case don't tell us a thing. In the first place the people of the South Tyrol had that plebiscite forced on them by what they consider to be two foreign governments—the Italians and the Germans. The people just wanted to stay here and to be left alone. But they were forced either to leave their homes if they wanted to keep their own language or customs, or to become Italian citizens if they didn't want to leave their own land. Of those who chose to leave, only a few were pro-Nazi: most of them had only a hatred of Italian domination. Of those who stayed, none of them considered they had become Italians; they played out the farce, stuck to their homes, and hated the Nazi for having forced this plebiscite. They knew they had been put between the devil and the deep blue sea. Then the Germans sent many of the exiled South Tyrolese away from the North Tyrol where they had expected to settle. That isn't being forgotten, either by those who stayed here, or by those who left here and were then cheated. When the Germans took over all the South Tyrol last September, all the Austrians were glad the Italians had gone. But many of them consider the Germans are just another gang of tyrants. And these are the people whom Mahlknecht has organized."

"And what about those who haven't been organized by Mahlknecht?" Shaw asked. "A lot have been coming back from the north this winter."

"These can be divided into two groups. The larger one hasn't done anything to help us so far, but they haven't helped the Germans either. They are waiting and watching. They are just pro-themselves. The smaller group is pro-German, because they still believe the German promises to save them from the Italians. They've seen the Germans replace the old Austrian names and inscriptions and Austrian is again being taught in the schools. They therefore believe that atrocity stories from other countries are merely propaganda, and some of them—who have returned from Germany, where they were made teacher's pets—think they are going to become powerful in key positions. Mahlknecht told us last night about some of these boys who are already Nazi bosses down in the bigger towns. Peter Hofer, for instance, in Bozen. He was killed in December. Karl Tinzl is still alive, though. Mahlknecht has a list of them.

They will be taken care of, either now as supposed air raid victims, or quite openly later when the need for secrecy is gone."

Thomson was smiling. "Peter Hofer was reported to have been killed in an air raid on Bozen," he said.

Shaw was thoughtful. "Mahlknecht and his friends have a difficult job. They haven't a clear-cut issue to put before their people: the Italian problem makes a mess of that. Did he tell you the Socialist underground paper, *Avanti,* has been having editorials showing that Italy must be given back the North Tyrol? It's Italy's historical function to protect the Brenner from the Germans."

"Swell job of protection they did when they got the chance," the American said. He gave a short laugh.

"It's a serious matter, though," Shaw said at last. "It's enough to throw all the South Tyrol into cynical neutrality."

"Not Mahlknecht or old Schroffenegger or any of their chaps!" Lennox said determinedly. He halted in amazement at the warmth of his own voice.

"I believe you," Shaw said. "Our men who made contact with him in Bozen saw some of his work there."

"All the more credit to these guys like Mahlknecht who do see the issue even if it's all blotted over for them. A lot of men won't fight unless they see things pure black and pure white," Thomson said. "Now, what interests me is just how Mahlknecht proposes to use his organization. What about that?"

"Yes," Shaw said. "We've learned why. But how?"

Lennox hesitated. He was gathering the facts together. He was worried in case he would forget the most important angles. Or perhaps the things which he thought important would not be what these two men wanted. That would be a criminal blunder on his part. They were waiting expectantly. That made him feel all the more nervous.

He began speaking too quickly.

"Take it easy," Thomson advised with that slow smile of his. "I'm kind of dumb." Shaw was smiling at that, and Lennox's tension eased. His explanation began to take concise form.

First of all, there was the German defense of the Brenner Pass and the Eisak Valley to be considered. That was the road into Austria. German guns, placed high on the mountainsides, would hold up any advance there by Allied troops for months. There would be wholesale slaughter. But men who knew the mountains, who had been supplied with the right equipment, could do an efficient job of sabotage. Some highly trained men should be sent into the mountains to help Mahlknecht's organization. It was willing and eager to do the job. It only needed a few experts— and a lot of explosives.

In the second place, there was the Allied attack. Parachutists, even gliders with air-borne troops, could land on the broad high meadows. If they were given excellent guides these advance units could cut off the narrow valley entirely and trap the German armies retreating from Italy.

Thirdly, there were political possibilities to be considered. The North Tyrol, where there was already much feeling against the Nazis, could have its resistance linked to the South Tyrol. Ties of blood and family were strong between the two districts. In action against the Germans they could achieve the union they had wanted. And if the North Tyrol were to rise—well, the North Tyrol bordered Bavaria. It was the biggest back door to Germany.

When he had ended the other two sat for some moments without speaking.

Lennox began to wonder if he had seemed a fool. He watched them nervously. They were looking at each other now, and he thought he saw an amused glance pass between them. Or perhaps it was a pleased glance. He hung on to that hope. Damn it all, what do they expect from a blasted amateur? he thought angrily.

Shaw said, "Ambitious, but exciting."

Thomson was grinning broadly. "At least, we won't be chasing our tail," he said. And Lennox suddenly realized that these two men had been as much afraid of being disappointed in his information as he had been afraid of their scorn.

The tension broke. The American rose, still smiling, and began pacing the floor. "Boy, it gives us some scope," he said at last. "I've got a couple of maps, but what about those guides you mentioned? One reliable guide is worth ten maps."

"Four members of the Committee are guides. That was their job in peacetime. And there are guides in every village. They know this country like the back of their hands."

"Have they much ammunition stored?" Shaw asked practically.

"No. They have small arms and a few machine guns which they swiped. They need more. And they need dynamite and grenades."

"What kind of man power?"

"They can't offer us quantity. They admit that. But they also say that you don't need numbers for fighting here. This is a place for infiltration, not massed attacks."

"Can they fight?"

"They are a fairly peaceful people. They are law-abiding and honest. But if they are roused they will fight. They are as hard as their mountains."

Shaw nodded thoughtfully, and then fell silent. He was thinking over what he had just heard. Thomson too was far away in a world of mountain contours and safe landing places.

Well, that's that, Lennox thought. He rose and walked to the doorway. He had given his report and his vote of confidence. His job was done. All he had to think of now was the road which would take him south into Italy. At last he could try that long-planned escape. Yet strangely, now that he could have it, he didn't want it. He glanced over his shoulder at the American and Englishman. He envied them.

He looked out over the grass—fine, thin grass, like the kind he used to see in a seedmonger's window display. There were small blue flowers close to the earth. A large flying beetle snapped its hard green wings at his feet. The small oaks, with their curiously gnarled trunks, were putting out their uneven leaves. The larch and spruce were tall and straight. They gave a blue cast to the depths of green in the woods. Soon the mountainside would be a stretch of bright color. The last snows on the tall gray mountain teeth would melt, and there would be peaches and vines ripening in the valleys under the high blue skies. "A poor country," Mahlknecht had said yesterday, but he had said it proudly. Now Lennox understood the simplicity of the people who lived here: they were content with little because they had so much.

He saw Mahlknecht leave Schroffenegger at the path into the wood, and start slowly towards the hut. He walked as a man who is worried and thoughtful.

Lennox turned quickly back into the hut. "There's still the problem of these two Jerries," he said quickly. "I had almost forgotten them."

Thomson and Shaw stopped their discussion.

"We can't get rid of them the easy way," Thomson said. "We can't have men with bullet- or knife-wounds lying about." Then thoughtfully: "We buried our parachutes according to the book. They might have heard our plane, might even—from some distance—have seen us drop. There's always that chance. But how did they connect all that with the Schichtl house?"

"They didn't connect it," Lennox suggested. "I don't believe they know you are here. You just timed your arrival for a rather delicate moment, that's all. They are looking for the men who guide Allied flyers out of these mountains. Johann disappears at certain periods and returns, exhausted but weather-beaten. Someone who knows

Johann well enough to note his disappearance and reappearance has given them that information. They have found that these disappearances take place after the remains of an Allied plane have been discovered. They are just checking up on Johann. That's all."

"But who could give that information about Johann?"

Lennox said, "He has been seeing a girl. Last thing on leaving, first thing on return, no doubt. She's the niece of a collaborationist. Mussner is the name."

"Johann's a bloody fool," Shaw said. He was angry. Thomson didn't seem any too pleased either. They both looked as if they had begun to wonder how many fools they might find on this job.

"No," Lennox said. "He isn't a fool. He's just young. He thinks that if a girl kisses you she really means it." Lennox was silent for a moment. He was too busy remembering the past to notice the American's uplifted eyebrow. "Perhaps he *was* a bloody fool," he concluded with a bitter smile, forcing himself away from the memories which he had thought were long buried.

Mahlknecht entered the room. He looked quickly at the two officers. "Well?"

"Everything is all right," Shaw answered. His Tyrolese accent wasn't too bad, Lennox noted. It would be perfect in a week or two. He couldn't resist feeling pleased that his own accent was better.

"Good." Mahlknecht was relieved. His whole face smoothed out. But his eyes were still thoughtful. "There is an immediate problem," he said.

The three younger men exchanged glances and smiled. "We know," Thomson agreed. "We were just discussing at this moment how to silence the two Germans and the Mussner girl."

"That can be managed." Mahlknecht's voice was quiet and capable. He was doing his best to keep the two newcomers' confidence in his people. It had been bad luck that the Germans' sudden interest in the Schichtl house had happened just at this time. Mahlknecht's pride was hurt: he had worked carefully, and now there was this incident which a stranger might think was a proof of incompetence. It showed Lennox somehow how sincerely Mahlknecht wanted the help of the Allies. He wanted these men to stay, to trust him and his people.

Mahlknecht was biting the corner of his lip again. When he spoke there was a certain dignity in his words. There was no minimizing of his worry.

"We can take care of the Mussner girl in a civilized manner," he said. "We shall send Johann away, with one of the missions into the North Tyrol. She will not see him again, so she will have no more guesses to pass over to her German friends. We shall watch her closely, from now on."

"And the two Jerries in the barn?" Shaw spoke crisply. He wasn't the man to make excuses, and he didn't expect any. He was a hard case, Lennox thought. That was the kind of man Mahlknecht had wanted; he had certainly got it.

"It would be easy to lead them up a mountain. There's many a way of getting rid of a man on a mountainside. But even if these Germans seemed to die accidentally on a mountain the question of why they should have been climbing is still unanswered. And other Germans, with stronger suspicions, would come and take their place. So the problem is this: we must lead them away from the Schichtl house back to where their friends can see them. And either we must put an end to their suspicions, or—if necessary—kill them. But on no account must their death confirm the Geman suspicion."

Shaw and Thomson nodded. They were pleased with Mahlknecht's quiet analysis. They were relieved that they weren't dealing with a hothead, filled with heroic plans which would only lead to disaster.

"You were right," Shaw said to Lennox. "Our friend Mahlknecht is a very careful fellow." Then he turned to

Mahlknecht. "What is your explanation of these waiting Germans?"

"First, they had some suspicion about the Schichtl house giving help to Allied airmen who had crashed. We believe that their suspicion came from vague information supplied by Eva Mussner. It must have been vague, or else we in the Schichtl house should all have been arrested yesterday. . . . Secondly, they must have learned that two men dropped from a plane near here last night. But they can have no idea whether these two men were parachuting as agents, or simply bailing out of a plane which might later have crashed in the high mountains. Certainly they have no idea who you are, for today, in the village, you were accepted by them as men of the Schlern. And that makes me believe, although we cannot be sure, that they are looking for two airmen rather than agents. . . . Thirdly, they went back to the Schichtl house, to see if the parachutists had gone there for help. The two Germans who are now dressed as civilians came along with the S.S. men because these civilians had seen us yesterday and so could identify any newcomers today."

"And that," Thomson said, "sounds as near the truth as we shall ever know. We'll have to work, as we've often done, by guess and by God. But the first problem is, they are still waiting."

Lennox said, "Yes. And why? They must have some real suspicion now about the Schichtl house." He kept worrying about the sure way in which the two Germans had walked to the Kasal barn. They had been settling down to watch and to wait. Of that he felt sure. "They found no strangers in the house. Why should they wait?"

"Perhaps," Mahlknecht said slowly, "perhaps they are waiting for you."

Lennox was silent. It was true: he hadn't been seen in the village, and so he should have been at the house. The Germans would think it interesting if he were to be found neither near the house nor in the village. He realized suddénly that this was the thought at the back of his mind which had been worrying him all afternoon. He realized that now as he listened to Mahlknecht's words. He knew what he had to do, what they expected him to do.

He moved over to the door so that he could see the grass and the trees and the mountains. He was wondering how you fought Germans with bare hands and quick wits. This was the civilian way of resisting; this was something new for a soldier to learn. A tommy gun would have seemed very comforting at this moment.

"I suppose I ought to move back to the house, then," he said. "The longer I stay away, the more questions they will begin to ask."

The others didn't answer. They were thinking of their other problems, balancing them against this one. They probably had a dozen worries to solve at this moment.

His voice became more assured. "Look, you have other things to think about. I'll shut up those two Jerries somehow. Johann will help me. Anyway, this looks like our particular headache."

The others accepted this solution.

"I'm glad you volunteered," Shaw said. "You'll manage it all right."

"If there's any questioning then act dumb," Thomson advised.

Lennox smiled grimly. "I shall be dumb, all right," he said. He was still wondering how to fight Germans with bare hands. And then it didn't seem so difficult: anyone who had been a prisoner of war had learned to fight with his wits.

Mahlknecht said, "Use your own judgment." And as Lennox looked at him sharply, he added, "—whether they stay alive or not."

Lennox nodded. He moved slowly over the clearing, and then as he saw Johann standing talking to old Schroffenegger at the path his pace quickened. Johann had won his bet. Katharina had been warned. Lennox was smiling as he said to the boy, "We have a little job to do."

The three men in the hut returned to the table.

Thomson straightened the map thoughtfully and picked up his pencil. "Pity we hadn't time to give them a helping hand."

The Englishman's silence showed he agreed.

Mahlknecht said slowly, "I am sorry, gentlemen, that this incident had to happen at this time." He was embarrassed as if he blamed himself for this complication.

The American laughed. "Don't let that worry you. Something always happens at the wrong time. Doesn't it, Roy?"

The Englishman nodded, absent-mindedly. "You know," he said, "that man Lennox might not be a bad chap to have around. Useful, perhaps."

"Yes," Thomson was thoughtful too. "Remember the colonel's report on him? Intelligent man, but undisciplined. Either Lennox has learned the hard way or the colonel was making a snap decision. I don't know of any greater discipline than being able to take your own orders."

"He's learned." Shaw paused, pretending to examine the map. "Now we had better get on with our own job. We'll have to trust Lennox to do his."

Mahlknecht sat astride a wooden bench, and began to advise. His own worry about Johann and Lennox began to recede: he began to believe, even as these two foreigners had assumed, that the Germans would have their problems too.

CHAPTER 17

The journey to the Schichtl house was swift. Johann's pace was steady and unbroken. He moved over the more difficult ground quickly, without slackening speed, as if he expected Lennox to follow easily. And because it was expected of him, Lennox managed it. Either the brief rest at Schönau, or the stimulus of the two Allied officers' arrival, or the sense of necessity which surrounded him had chased away the fatigue of his muscles. Or perhaps they had never really forgotten the long months of training in the desert. They were obeying him, anyway. His mind was clear. He had a feeling of growing confidence. He was sure now that the job which he and Johann had to do could be done, if only they were quick enough at improvising. Improvise, he told himself—that's your best chance.

As he followed Johann's easy stride, imitating its changes in rhythm, matching footholds down difficult terrain, he could let his mind think about the simplest plan on which improvisation could be worked. He kept remembering Mahlknecht's implication. The Germans were first to be satisfied that he was alone at the house that he didn't, expect anyone. Then they were to be led away from the house. They were to be led away. And after that he was to use his own judgment.

The sunlight was deepening in color. A cool breeze was blowing up from the meadows. From the direction of the village he could hear the gay, distant music of a band, ebbing and flowing like a tide as the wind dropped or strengthened. The late afternoon had brought high clouds, tight and withdrawn into the soft blue of the sky. The rock of the mountain precipices had lost its hard gray look: the yellow sun was drawing out the warmth from its veins. The dark fir trees grew more secret with the coming of evening; the thick stretches of woods, like twisting bands of rich green velvet, separated the bright new grass in the meadows from the giant teeth of rock. Lennox thought of the men and women gathered together in the village, of their gay costumes and bright music and friendly laughter disguising nagging worries. He thought of the Germans in the village and the hidden trucks, quietly waiting. He thought of the three men in the forester's hut on the Schönau; of old Schroffenegger guarding the south path while his two sons kept watch on the northern road to the lumber camp. He thought of Johann and himself moving on their grim errand across the wide mountainside. The background of space and height gave the feeling of peace. It was a most noble illusion, he decided bitterly.

At the wood behind the Schichtl house they avoided the path, and made their way carefully and indirectly down between the thicker trees. Halfway Lennox stopped to give his quiet instructions. Johann nodded; he was listening intently. His young face was strangely blank. But the plan seemed to please him, for he nodded again and clapped Lennox's shoulder as much as to say, "We'll give the blighters a run for their money." Then he cut swiftly off to his left to reach the edge of the wood where Katharina and Lennox had watched the German car on the road. Lennox walked on to the house.

The untouched breakfast table reminded him that he was hungry. The fire in the stove was almost out. The house was forlorn and cheerless, as if it remembered the disordered bedroom upstairs, the neglect downstairs, and resented such unusual treatment.

He decided to attend to the fire first. It was something

of a job to get it lit if he once let it die out completely. He raked the ashes gently, threw on some small dried twigs, and then decided to go out for more wood. The logs were piled outside under the windows. Here was the chance for anyone watching this house to see him being thoroughly domestic. He felt self-conscious about the way he wouldn't let himself look at the Kasal barn. And then he wondered suddenly whether the Germans were still there. He'd feel a fool if they weren't, pretending so hard to be so damned natural. He brought back two logs into the house, carrying them in his left arm. He hoped his right arm would look weak to any observer. He made a second journey, and a third, using only his left arm for the carrying.

After that he felt he deserved an outsized sandwich. He ate it, standing at the side of the neat window with its crisp curtains, keeping his body well out of sight of the road. He was wondering just what the two Germans were planning now; they must have identified him from the Kasal barn, and yet they themselves couldn't come over here to question him. It gave him some pleasure to think that life was complicated for them too. If anything he had the advantage over them: the Germans were watching him, but they didn't know that they themselves were being just as carefully watched. His vigil at the window was rewarded. He saw one of the men leave the Kasal barn, moving quickly round its side so that he could no longer be seen from the Schichtl house or the road. He didn't appear again: he must have gone down into the low-lying field where his movements would be hidden. Lennox heard the Kasal dog bark. The German must be walking past the lean cows at pasture. Well, that was one way of reaching Hinterwald quietly and making a report. The other must still be waiting in the barn. How both of them must have cursed the simplicity of life in these mountains: a telephone in the Kasal farmhouse would have been a useful gadget at this moment. Anyway, Lennox thought as he turned away from the window, he had ruined a fine May afternoon for them. He hoped they had run out of cigarettes, too.

He poured some milk, cut another slice of bread and another chunk of cold meat, and sat down at the table with a feeling of satisfaction. The next move was the Germans', and he guessed it wouldn't take long. He had made the opening gambit. This whole business was, the more he thought of it, rather like a game of chess. It was a damned queer way to fight a war. Yet this was the way it was being fought by a lot of people. He wondered how many women and men in Europe were at this moment waiting for a German to come and question them.

He had finished his second glass of milk, and was making a third sandwich, when he heard the approaching car. So the German, slinking across the fields, had reached Hinterwald and recruited strength. And now the test. He imagined Johann at this moment, alert, watchful. Probably sweating it out. Lennox wasn't exactly cool and collected himself. But he would have to be. . . . Lack of confidence was an expensive luxury when you paid with your life. Prison camp had taught him to be an actor, a dissembler. He had faced questioning before; all he had to do, he knew, was to stick to his story.

He began eating the sandwich. He sat down once more, sprawling with his feet resting on a second chair. He unbuttoned his waistcoat, and propped the German-published *Bozener Tageblatt* against the earthenware crock of milk at his elbow. The haggled loaf spread its coarse crumbs on the tablecloth. The remains of meat looked as if it had been enjoyed. Lennox studied the effect and was satisfied. The observant German eyes, which would mark every detail, would see a picture of a bucolic bachelor enjoying the simple pleasures of home.

The car halted outside the house. Peter Lennox looked up from his newspaper as the front door was pushed open.

The two Germans, in the black uniform of special police,

whom he had already seen today, were standing in the doorway.

Lennox stopped chewing and surveyed them gravely.

"This the road to Seis?" one of them asked.

Lennox nodded with deliberation. "Yes," he said. "Yes, it's one of the roads to Seis." He ignored the prying eyes. He went on eating. "There's a better road down on the meadows."

"Have you been here all day?"

"Mostly."

"Did you see two men following this road?"

Lennox shook his head.

"Are you sure?" While the one man questioned the other looked round the kitchen intently. He didn't learn anything there, for he moved back into the living room. It seemed to Lennox that he was staring at the steps leading up to the bedroom.

"I didn't notice anyone while I was here," Lennox said with determination through a well-filled mouth. He chewed reflectively.

"You were down at the village?"

"No. I was out for a walk this afternoon. Went to get a breath of air."

"Did you see a car?"

"I heard a car just after I left the house. Couldn't see it, though."

"Were you away from this house for long?"

"Not so very long. An hour or two. Perhaps three. Time passes quickly."

"Three hours looking at the view?" The German's voice was losing any patience it had adopted initially.

"I fell asleep." Lennox's voice was friendly and confiding. "There's a good place under a pine tree. The sun was warm. And the view was good."

"Enjoying life, aren't you?" There was no humor in the hard eyes.

Lennox finished the sandwich and then looked up at the German. "There were no mountains to look at in Africa," he said. "There wasn't much sleep either."

The other German was standing at the entrance to the house. His head was bent as if he were studying the gleam on his well-polished boots.

"So you're an old soldier. Got your papers?" the cross-examining German asked. Lennox produced them. The German read them with interest.

"From the Zittertal, eh? You're quite a way from home."

"I've no home there any more. I came here because my aunt could give me one until I got well again."

The German didn't answer. He was now studying Peter Schichtl's discharge papers. He glanced quickly at Lennox's right hand. The scar reassured him, for he went on reading with less interest. Severe wound in right hand, shrapnel fragments in right forearm, bullet wound close to left lung and possible weakness of lung.

The German threw the papers on the table. "Report with these at the police station," he said. "All men are to register there."

Lennox stared stupidly.

The German said impatiently, "The police station in Hinterwald."

As Lennox still said nothing, still sat staring, the German said with rising anger, "Report at police headquarters. At the Golden Roof Inn. Today. Understand?"

Lennox gathered up his papers slowly, put them carefully away, rose, and searched for his hat, and nodded.

The German, who was waiting at the door, said "Nothing here. Come on." He moved out into the sunlight.

The German who had done the talking followed him. They didn't speak within Lennox's hearing. He heard the car start, and saw it follow ostensibly the track to Seis. He was quite prepared to wager that it would swing west on the first crossroads it met, and circle round by the "foreigners' road" towards Hinterwald again. The Germans were concentrating on Hinterwald today.

He cleared the table so that the littered kitchen wouldn't upset Frau Schichtl on her return. The stove was burning slowly with the new wood. The logs he hadn't used were drying on the whitewashed stone hearth. Before he left the house he paused as the curious German had done, and looked at the staircase. The steps were perfectly normal, practical wooden steps scrubbed white. But as he looked he had a sudden doubt. The four bottom steps were less white, as if a dust film were over them. He bent down and drew a finger along the surface of the lowest step. There was a whitish powder on his forefinger. He walked up the four steps and then walked down again. The dust had clung to his shoes, and there was the faint but clear outline of their soles. He crossed over to the front door. The same fine powder had been scattered over the threshold, for the impression of the Germans' boots was there. Not strong, but definite enough if you were looking for it. At the back door, he found the marks of many footsteps, but it was plain they came from the one pair of shoes— his shoes. Anyone coming into this house, carefully, cleverly, to avoid the Germans would have still been caught; anyone hidden in a secret place upstairs which the Germans hadn't been able to discover in their search, anyone venturing downstairs when he thought the house was empty, would have been discovered.

Lennox was not exactly cheerful as he left the house and started to walk towards the village. He was too angry with himself for having taken so long to notice the German trick, a petty trick, a silly trick. But still a trick which might have come off. He reflected that when he had been a prisoner of war he had been sharp-witted enough to notice that kind of thing, or at least to have suspected something like it. He had learned the old lesson once more this afternoon: expect nothing, trust nothing. Fortunately the Schichtls and Mahlknecht hadn't been so simple-minded as the Germans had thought. There had been no strangers as secret guests in the house.

He passed the Kasal barn, and then the farmhouse. Johann, from his vantage point in the woods, must have seen him on this stretch of road; and he would know that all was well so far. And Johann would now be keeping a steady pace on the higher mountain path to Hinterwald, so that he would reach there before Lennox did, and would be standing at the doorway of the Hotel Post to welcome his "cousin." They had chosen the Post as their meeting place, for it lay at the beginning of the village, and Lennox would see it very easily. Besides, the owner of the hotel was a trusted friend of Mahlknecht.

The Kasals' dog barked. But there was no other noise or movement from the farm buildings. As he followed the twisted road, and knew that he was now hidden from view from the Kasal barn, Lennox began to walk more briskly. His movements felt natural once more, now that no German eyes were watching him.

The first stage was over: he had made his claim that he had been near the house all day, and that he had been alone. There was no evidence, yet, to disprove that. The second stage was now beginning: the Germans were to be drawn away from the Schichtl house. The solitary German, now left in the barn, must have seen Lennox take the road to Hinterwald. There were two things the German could do. Either he could keep right on sitting in the barn, and much good that would do him watching an empty house, or he could set out to follow his suspect to Hinterwald. "Don't look now, but . . ." Lennox told himself. He began to whistle one of Frau Schichtl's favorite songs.

His spirits mounted as he thought of the three men— the German, Johann, and himself—all traveling to Hinterwald by parallel routes: Johann up on the hillside, he on the cart track, the German no doubt using the shortcut across the fields. It amused him still more that the Germans were under a pretty delusion: they didn't know that within this last hour their whole function had changed. They had become just as much the hunted as they had been the hunters.

CHAPTER 18

The road began to wind downhill like a snake basking in sunshine. Evening was drawing near. The cool breeze on the hillside gave way to the still air of the valley. Sounds were magnified. The music was stronger now: Lennox could hear the clear notes of a trumpet and the deeper tones of a trombone. The drum beat out the first pulse in a gay three-to-the-bar tune.

He passed four large summer villas, shuttered and abandoned, hiding their loneliness among scattered trees. Then there was a small meadow, falling in a gentle curve towards the village. A small church, no longer than forty feet, had been built on top of the meadow. The wooden spire, rising from the square tower, was onion-shaped. The plaster walls had been colored, and they had weathered into a faded pink. There were wide-spaced paintings of saints, which decorated without concealing the walls' surface. Lennox noted that the balance of the design was good. He slowed his pace, and then suddenly climbed the short slope of grass towards the church. He began walking round its outside walls.

Some of the murals showed definite training and talent, some were more primitive. Those on the south wall had almost disappeared under sun and rain. There were cracks in the wall too now that he examined it closely. This church was poor: little money had been spent on it in recent years. Above the door was the figure of Christ on the Cross. The loincloth was painted white, and the flesh tone was dark brown. The artist had captured a strangely pitying look in the large, gentle eyes. Lennox's interest quickened.

He hesitated on the worn stone step. The inside of the church was in shadow, for the windows were high-placed on the walls. There was a pyramid of candles burning with a clear, steady flame on the small altar. Behind it was an elaborately carved wooden triptych. Lennox took a step forward. It was as if the last five years of his life had vanished in as many minutes.

There was the rustle of silk and the light sound of narrow heels. A woman came out of the church. She pulled back the embroidered scarf which had covered her smooth dark hair, and let it fall around her shoulders as a shawl. She was young. Her low-necked black dress was of rich silk banded with velvet. The wide sleeves of her blouse, very white above the black lace which covered her forearms, were transparent and crisp. Her flower-embroidered apron was of a curiously clear blue. It matched the color of her eyes.

She looked at him in surprise for a moment. But she recovered first. *"Grüss Gott!"* she said.

"Grüss Gott!" he answered slowly. He was watching her, with the background of gleaming candles behind the dark head, with the faded pink walls framing the slender figure in its elaborate costume.

"There is no one in the church. Father Strum had to leave—he was needed at Seis. Frau Kaufmann is dying."

"In that case," Lennox began awkwardly, and moved away from the church door. He didn't finish his sentence. He remembered that Hinterwald shared its old Austrian priest with several other small villages. The Tyrolese were deeply Catholic, but they had never attended the larger church which the Italians had built to the south of Hinterwald, even if it were in good repair and had a priest who lived beside it. For the Italian functionaries and their families and the summer visitors had worshiped there. And as long as the name of Hinterwald had been struck off

the map to give way to the alien Montefierro, as long as
the children at school were forced to speak in a foreign
language, as long as a man could be arrested for whistling
a Tyrolese song in public, these Austrians of the South
Tyrol had avoided the well-provided church at the other
end of the village. That, reflected Lennox, was something
for the future peacemakers and map drawers to remember
about human beings.

The girl had been speaking. Lennox said, "Please?"
politely. He noticed, with approval, the high cheekbones
and the almost classical line of nose and chin. The texture
of her skin was smooth, its color was vivid and alive.
Beauty, when it is natural, is overpowering.

"Are you going to the village?" she asked for the second
time. She was smiling now.

"Yes."

"Then we can walk together." She wasn't smiling any
more. In repose, there was a certain sadness, almost a
tenseness, in her face. She looked sideways at him as he
fell into step beside her.

"I didn't see you there this morning." Her voice was
polite.

"No. I have only just arrived."

"You are a stranger?"

"I'm Frau Schichtl's nephew. Peter Schichtl. Before the
war I lived in the Zittertal."

"Then you are Johann's cousin." The warmth of her
voice should have warned him, but he was still watching
that line of throat and chin.

"Yes."

"Why did you come to the South Tyrol?"

"I've no home left up north. My mother died while I
was in the Army." He thought grimly of the double meaning to his words. His people had indeed died while he
was in the Army—a land mine in Chiswick had blotted out
everything that had formed his home.

"Your brothers and sisters?"

"Scattered. I don't know where they are." Again it was bitterly true. The war had altered a lot of things.

"Are you here on leave from the Army?"

"Discharged." And that would probably be true, too. The murals on the church wall had reminded him of his hand. If he couldn't hold a pencil he couldn't hold a gun. He'd be discharged, all right. The bitterness in his voice reached the girl, for she was silent.

"You are sorry you are no longer in the Army?" she asked after a pause.

"Yes," he replied shortly. He noticed a shade of disappointment pass over her face. She looked at him coldly, almost accusingly. And he remembered, as he felt the first blight of disapproval, that she had been referring to the German Army.

After that she fell silent. They were walking on the road now, and on either side were scattered houses built among the trees which encircled Hinterwald. Then suddenly the road became a village street. There was a fountain, with the gaily colored wooden figure of a child holding an emptying pitcher out of which the water fell in a thin arc. There was a row of white houses winding downhill, with their carved wooden balconies and broad gable ends turned towards the street. Other houses were scattered in depth behind those on the street. None were in a straight row—the broad, flat roofs angled in every direction. There was a feeling of independence in the disarray of houses which were, in themselves, so well-designed and neat.

Lennox heard the voices of children, and their laughter. Ahead of him was the band, and people listening to the music. He halted. The girl stopped walking too, and watched him curiously. It was difficult for him to pretend to be as placid as these groups of oldish men who talked so quietly together, their weather-beaten faces impassive under the white-plumed hats. It had been nearly three years since he had seen a crowd of people enjoying themselves, since he had seen so many women gathered together.

The young girls stood like a cluster of blond statues, tall and broad-shouldered. Their hands were folded in front of the wide, deep layers of their skirts, as they gravely watched the red-faced musicians. Their restraint, their quietness, emphasized the strength of their bodies. Some older women stood behind the girls and watched them carefully, proudly. The children, with fair hair bleached silver, darted about among the spreading skirts and bright silk aprons, pursuing mysterious games, laughing for no obvious reason at all. He had forgotten how children could laugh. Over nothing.

Lennox's throat tightened, and there was a pinpricking behind his eyes. Bloody hell, he thought, and looked quickly away from the people to the inanimate houses. This girl beside him wasn't going to see him turn sentimental. He stared fixedly at the wall of the nearest house. And there, under a coat of white paint he could see the dimmed outlines of giant black lettering which had once greeted those arriving in the village. It was the Fascist slogan: *Crédere— Obbedire—Combattere.* Believe, obey, fight. Lennox's eyes hardened. He was in complete control again. It took more than a coat of paint, he was thinking, to obliterate that memory.

The girl said quietly, "We left it still showing. It's our monument to remind us of what the Fascists did to our village." She was watching his expression, and she became more friendly. "If you didn't come down to see the procession this morning why do you come down now? You shouldn't have come. See, there are few young men here now."

"I was sent down here. Two Germans came to the house and told me to come. I have to register at the police station."

"So here you are—just like that!" She stared at him in

scorn and amazement. And then she was alarmed. "They came to the *Schichtl* house?"

He looked at her in some surprise. "Yes."

"What did they want?"

"I don't know. They asked questions, and then they went away. I don't know."

The girl looked at him as if he were a complete fool. He had to admit he had tried to give the impression. And then he saw she was angry because she was afraid.

"Was Johann with you?"

"No. He's in the village."

"He isn't. He hasn't been here all afternoon." The lovely face was tense with worry. "Can I trust you?" she asked suddenly, pathetically. "Johann is in danger. These two Germans came to question him. He's in danger, and it is my fault."

Lennox was looking at her so uncomprehendingly that she began an urgent, rambling explanation. Her voice was low as if she were afraid that a passer-by might overhear; it was hurried as if she knew there was little time. She had trusted her uncle. She had not seen him for a long time except for his two visits to Bozen at Christmas and Easter, for when their house in Hinterwald had been closed he had gone to live in the North Tyrol. She had preferred to stay in Bozen with her cousins. When he visited them it seemed natural that he should ask news about their old village, about the people she was meeting in Bozen. And she had, without thinking, answered his questions about Johann Schichtl.

When she finished Lennox was staring at her.

She misinterpreted his expression. "Do you understand what I mean? You must warn Johann. He avoided me today. You will tell him?"

Lennox smiled slowly, "You are mistaken," he said. "Johann isn't in danger. He has done nothing to put himself in danger. What danger is there?"

The blue eyes looked at him in anger. "You are a fool," she said.

He avoided her gaze. "Yes?" he asked quietly. He was looking down the village street again. At the door of the Hotel Post he saw Johann. And beyond, at a safe distance, he saw two men lounging against a wall. They were listening to the band which was now marching determinedly, if somewhat exhaustedly, towards the Hotel Post's garden. Their heads had turned away from him, but he knew that they had seen him. They were dressed in ordinary clothes, of the color and shape which he had seen entering the Kasal barn this afternoon. So he had brought them back to the village, and away from the Schichtl house. At least, he had managed the second stage of the job.

He looked once more at the girl, and smiled generously. He was thinking of all the German tricks. He couldn't have played a safer game than to look a fool. Her report to her uncle and his Nazi friends would give him a lot of comfort.

He was surprised to see her anger give way to tears. She said again, with difficulty, "Please tell Johann."

"Tell him yourself. He's over there," Lennox nodded to the door of the Hotel Post.

She looked, and she was obviously surprised. And then she shook her head. "He will avoid me if I go over, as all the others have been avoiding me." She turned towards him and said bitterly, "Why do you think I was in the church this afternoon? I'll tell you. I was running away from eyes in the street. Eyes which dislike me. That's why I was in the church." Her voice changed again. It was almost lifeless now. "Once I had friends here. When I came back here from Bozen I thought I would be happy. But I found today that I was mistaken. I've been mistaken in many things, it seems. My uncle—Won't you believe me? Have you never known someone you loved and trusted, someone who was separated from you for five years whom you still loved and trusted? And then you found that, although he looked the same, spoke the same, seemed the same, he had changed here"—she placed her clenched fist over her heart—"and here?" Her hand went to her brow.

Lennox was quite motionless. His voice was cold and hard. "It doesn't take five years. Six months is long enough with some women."

The girl was watching him. She was neither curious nor angry any more. She touched his arm gently for a moment.

"I'm sorry," she said, so quietly that he could hardly hear her words. "You do know, then, that I speak the truth." She wondered what woman had changed in six months to hurt this man so deeply. Perhaps when he was away at the war. It would hurt most then.

He left her suddenly, as if he had read her thoughts.

She would have run after him, even if the whole village had laughed at her. But her uncle, sober-faced, soberly dressed in ordinary town clothes, was coming towards her. She waited, wondering what he would have to say now.

Johann took his hands out of his tight pockets, and removed the weight of his shoulder from the inn door. But he did not look at Lennox. His eyes looked beyond, to the street. "That was Eva Mussner," he said.

Lennox nodded.

Johann was still watching. "Her uncle has reached her," he reported. "They are talking. . . . She is walking with him. . . . They are going towards the Mussner house. And our two German snoopers are moving towards it too, and they've reached it, and they've gone inside. The Mussners have now reached the house also. . . . They've entered it. . . ." His voice was bitter. In his heart he had defended Eva Mussner, even if he had accepted his family's judgment for security's sake. In his heart he had hoped he could find proof that his family was wrong. And here was proof of another kind. The girl and her uncle had followed the two Germans into the Mussner house, as if by some prearranged plan. No doubt the Germans had thought of it, and given Mussner his instructions when they had seen the Schichtls' cousin talking so seriously with the girl.

Johann said roughly, "Come on. My mother and Frau Kasal are waiting for us. Come on."

Lennox still had nothing to say. He had resisted the momentary temptation to turn and look at the Mussner house. For all he knew, the Germans might be now watching from its windows to see how interested Johann and he were. Well, they weren't interested. Johann and he were now entering the inn.

Johann led the way. In the dark, wood-paneled, flag-stoned hall he said, "What's wrong with you? Did you tell Eva Mussner too much?" He smiled derisively. "She's easy to talk to, isn't she?"

"She learned nothing."

Lennox pretended to look at the carved design on the nearest panel. It represented a harvesting scene, with thick stacks of rye ready for the miller and rich vines heavy with grapes for the wine press. The artist had dated his work 1771. Lennox kept looking at the date. He was seeing it, but he wasn't even thinking about it: it was just something to fix his eyes on, to avoid looking at Johann.

"Tell me, Johann," he said very quietly, "do you think she is with her uncle in this?"

Johann said gruffly, "She's certainly with him at this moment."

Lennox stopped looking at the carved panel. The two men eyed each other carefully. But they said nothing more.

In the little wine room some of the older men and women were resting. Tired children sat obediently beside their grandparents. Their small, fair heads leaned back against the paneled walls, and their short legs stuck out numbly from the broad high benches. Above them the wooden panels were carved out into elaborate hunting scenes, but the children were too weary even to look at the stags and the chamois. Their bodies drooped with temporary exhaustion. For once they were silent, and only asked questions with their eyes.

Frau Schichtl had chosen one of the long tables, and beside her—talking worriedly, seriously—was a thin-faced woman who was evidently Frau Kasal. There were others at the table too, but they had grouped round Frau Schichtl and they were talking so continuously that they scarcely noticed the two young men beyond a polite phrase of greeting and a dignified bow. Usually a stranger would have excited interest. But today the people of the village were too occupied in hiding their worries by argument among themselves. They had too many questions of their own, still unanswered. Young Schichtl and his cousin seated themselves at the unoccupied end of the table. They seemed, outwardly, to belong to this party of peasants; actually, they were as isolated as if they had had a small table of their own. And they were less noticeable this way. Johann's next words confirmed that. With his elbow on the table, and his chin cupped in his hand so that the movement of his lips were scarcely noticeable, he said, "We can talk here."

"Give me five minutes," Lennox answered. Johann nodded, and became absorbed in ordering some wine.

Peter Lennox slumped on the hard bench as completely as the children. He would rest for five minutes and let his body relax completely. Then he would start shaping the plan which had begun to exist in his mind. For he must have a solid, simple plan; he must have a basis on which he could improvise, as he had been told to do. That was his job.

Around him was the constant rise and fall of voices. He watched the black flies circling aimlessly above the wooden table, and listened to their steady humming. Frau Schichtl and her friends were talking, but he heard nothing. He tried to think about nothing, too. But he kept thinking of Eva Mussner. She knew all the tricks, he decided bitterly. And then he was conscious that Johann was refilling his glass with wine, that Johann was waiting with eager impatience. Lennox pushed aside his glass, and rested his elbows on the table. He didn't look at Johann. He was watching the others, as if what they were discussing interested him. Johann was studying the jerky progress of a thirsty fly, as it scouted round the edge of some spilled wine.

Lennox began to talk, speaking in the old prison-camp way, his voice low, his lips scarcely moving.

CHAPTER 19

The band had finished drinking its beer in the garden of the Hotel Post, and had begun to play once more. It seemed as if these people couldn't have enough of their simple, lighthearted music. But then, this was the first village festival for twenty-five years at which the old Tyrolese songs were allowed to be played in public without threat of fine or imprisonment. The wine room had emptied. The children went out holding their grandmothers' hands, and the old men followed to sit in the garden and listen to their music.

Frau Schichtl had gone too. As she left the table she had come round to where her son and Peter Lennox were sitting, and she had paused long enough to say in a low voice, "Take good care of each other." She placed her hand for a moment on their shoulders. Lennox realized, as she had already done, that he might never see her again.

The empty room gathered its shadows. From the darkening garden came the lilt of a light-stepping air. No one was dancing yet, as if the people were trying to postpone it.

When darkness came, Lennox thought, there would have to be plenty of dancing. The older men and women would pretend it was quite normal that the younger men were no longer there. And the girls would dance with each other, as if they were enjoying themselves, as if it didn't matter that there were no young men to dance with. And those who were determined not to believe any wild rumors about German trucks would blame the suspicious young men for having ruined the festival. All of those people

161

were facing an evening which their stubborn highland
pride would not let them abandon. Some of them hoped to
cover the absence of the younger men, to give them enough
time to reach the huts scattered high over the mountains.
Others were going to stay to prove that the hotheads were
wrong with this whispered talk of danger. But none of
them had a real sense of disaster: tonight was only a repeating pattern to the people of Hinterwald. Once the
Italians had come hunting young men too, and when there
were no young men to be found the Italians had gone away.
The village had been fined. That was all. These people had
not yet learned that the Germans are more persevering,
more thorough, and more ruthless than the Italians.

When darkness came, Lennox thought, Johann and he
must be ready. He had already explained his plan to the
boy beside him, and the main points—the timing and
place of their action—had been decided. Only one problem remained. The room had remained empty, and the
hotelkeeper—he could be trusted—had stationed himself
in the hall. When darkness came, Lennox thought once
more, he and Johann would be moving quietly to the road
which led away from this village to Kastelruth. For although the Tyrolese might think that the trucks would roll
away empty if there were no younger men to fill them,
Lennox wasn't so sure about that. He knew the Germans
better than these people did: he had seen what they could
do when all disguises were down.

Johann was trying to find a solution to that last problem.
He was biting his lip in a beardless imitation of Mahlknecht.

"No telephone wire anywhere?" Lennox asked again.
"Surely somewhere, Johann."

"We should have to strip the telephone poles. No time.
What about rope?"

"Not strong enough." Lennox was worried. It showed in
his eyes, and the impatient tapping of his fingers on the

table. The last detail was a small one, but unless it were perfect, his whole plan would be useless.

"Or a tree across the road would block them. That would give those in the trucks a chance to escape. If you could find a gun we could divert the soldiers' attention. They would think it was an ambush," Lennox said. He was thinking out loud now, but even as he spoke he knew that this alternative suggestion was no good.

Up on Schönau Mahlknecht had said that for the moment there must be no obvious evidence of violence. And the two officers had agreed; for German retaliation and restrictions would make their work twice as difficult, twice as slow. At this stage of the organizing of resistance it would be better that no action were taken by Johann and Lennox if that action meant open trouble for Shaw's and Thomson's plans now being made at Schönau. Lennox suddenly realized that they had given him a pretty big responsibility: it was up to him entirely to keep a balance—to do neither too much nor too little.

Johann said, "I don't see why it isn't strong enough. It is strong enough, certainly, not to be sawed through by the edge of rock."

Lennox stared. "Mountaineering rope, you mean?"

"Of course. What else? We've plenty of it in the village. It has wire woven through its center."

Wire through the center? That might do. Lennox said, "What about its color? It is almost white, isn't it? Can you get any dark paint or stain?"

"This is the season for painting shutters and window boxes, isn't it?" Johann was smiling now. Their plan was beginning to look simple once more. I'll attend to it right away, eh? It won't take long. I'll meet you at the trees just southwest of the church, beside St. Johann's shrine. In half an hour—as soon as the dance starts.

"How long will it take us to reach the part of the road you've chosen for the accident?"

"By shortcuts, about fifteen or twenty minutes. Maybe

less. By the road itself, it would take us three times as long as that. The road winds to avoid hilly ground." Johann's hand traced the road's curves through the air as he spoke.

"Good. You are sure that part of the road is suitable?"

"Sure? It is what you described, isn't it?" Johann was beginning to get impatient. Lennox decided not to say, "Perhaps we shouldn't take any of this action. It is on our own authority. Perhaps we have done enough already. Perhaps the trucks will return empty to Kastelruth, after all." For Johann would have been too disappointed. He would have thought that Lennox did not really want action, or even that a doubtful plan was not worth preparing. No; better let Johann keep his excitement and his energy. Any qualification on the plan at this moment would only dampen the boy's enthusiasm. It would only lead to disappointment and resentment.

"In half an hour," Lennox said.

The hotelkeeper straightened his shoulders, moved away from the door, and had a short attack of coughing. Someone must have entered the hall from the street. Lennox and Johann exchanged glances. Johann's hand traveled to his waist, where he kept his sheathed knife. Lennox was calculating the distance to the kitchen entrance to the room; there would be a back exit through there. Even if the inn had been surrounded the number of people gathered in its garden would make escape possible. You could lose yourself in a crowd.

But the person who entered was a woman. She stood very still at the threshold of the room, as if she were trying to identify them in the dusk. She seemed satisfied, and came forward into the room.

"Why don't you turn on the light?" she asked. "I nearly missed you." It was Eva Mussner.

Johann rose abruptly. The wooden bench scraped angrily on the floor as he pushed it aside, and he walked past the girl without even looking at her.

"You see," she said to Lennox, "I have lost my friends."

He rose too. He walked towards the hall. Johann had already vanished. In half an hour he would be waiting. In half an hour Lennox would have to decide what Mahlknecht and his two visitors would want him to do.

Eva Mussner caught his arm as he passed her.

"Please," she said. "Please."

She had dropped her voice, until it was almost a whisper. "I have something to tell you. Not here. This isn't a good place: no one could talk of secret things here. Let us go outside, and pretend to be watching the alpine glow. Please."

She was walking beside him. He pretended to agree. He was planning to lose her in the crowd, quietly, effectively: that was the best treatment.

She said, "They sent me to talk to you. They want to know more about you."

He halted for a moment, looking down at her.

"You are all wasting a lot of breath," he said brutally. But he had changed his mind about losing this girl in the crowd. He wanted to hear what she had been told to tell him. And he wanted her to repeat to "them" what he wanted them to believe.

The street was still more crowded. People were coming out of the houses, out of the other inns. They were walking slowly towards the Hotel Post. Soon the dance would begin.

The girl drew close to his side, and guided him towards the house at the beginning of the street where the obliterated Fascist slogan stood. It was less crowded here, as if the people disliked this end of the street. The girl walked slowly now, and she began to speak, quickly, quietly. Both of them seemed to be watching the sun's last rays reflecting on the high mountain walls. The sun was almost set, and the air had lost all its light, but the peaks of gray rock came to life. They glowed with the rich fire of rubies. The sun disappeared, even as Lennox watched, and the village became a place of deep twilight with white ghostlike houses. The mountain walls had turned to opals. In the dark sky they glowed with the sunlight they had trapped and still held. They shone with the changing, blending shades of gold and purple and rose. There was stillness over the village as everyone, standing in the first darkness of night, turned to watch the alpine glow.

The girl was watching too. She was speaking, and her voice was unsteady as if she had been tortured at the sight of the glowing mountains.

"The Germans have trucks outside the village. And soldiers. They have been waiting all day for the signal when everyone is gathered together."

He said nothing. He hoped she would think his face, if she could see it clearly, was registering doubt.. But he was thinking that she couldn't have chosen a more clever opening. She was establishing confidence by news which was no news.

When he didn't answer she said quickly, "They've decided the dance will be the best time. They need volunteers. Men."

"Do they?"

She ignored his sarcasm. "They are angry. A police station was set up here today. Notices were posted. But no one has registered. Only my uncle has been what they call, polite. And they began to notice, in this last hour, that the young men have left the village. They are angry and worried. They are beginning to ask questions. They asked me about you."

"And you said?" The mountain colors were infused with streaks of indigo, turning the rose color to a violet-red. The sky above, the forests below, were almost black.

"That you were a stupid country bumpkin, and that you hadn't become any less stupid in the Army."

In spite of himself, he was annoyed. "Thank you for the compliment."

"I also said I had known you for a long time, that you came to Bozen on leave."

He didn't reply at once to that. He was too busy thinking he couldn't blame Johann for having trusted this girl. There was a sincerity in her voice which was disarming.

"And why did you say that?" he asked coldly.

"Oh, please!" The girl was almost in tears now. "No man can be so stupid that he doesn't see the dangers staring him in the face."

Lennox kept silent. Blindness doesn't only attack fools, he thought grimly.

She said, "Listen, you've got to believe me. Listen. They have been ordered to treat us with velvet gloves so that we'll collaborate easily. They don't want to stir up any more trouble at the moment. The news has just come that Cassino has fallen, that the German Army is withdrawing. Rome will fall too."

Lennox was standing very still now. But he wasn't looking any longer at the glowing mountains suspended in darkness. She sensed she had won some reaction, for she was speaking still more urgently. "But what if they find no one who will collaborate with them except men like my uncle? They have begun talking, up at my uncle's house, about how firm they can allow themselves to be. They have decided that if they can find no men to volunteer they will take women and children and hold them as hostages at Kastelruth, until the young men come down from their hiding places in the mountains to volunteer."

"And when is this to happen?"

"At eight o'clock."

Eight o'clock. That was earlier than he had thought the Germans would act. They must be worried. He asked, more casually than he felt, "And what am I supposed to do?"

"You could tell Frau Schichtl—Johann—anyone who could pass the word round. You could warn the village, let everyone know, let everyone go away."

"And what about the people who live in this village?

What are they to do? Will your uncle defend them against reprisals?"

She ignored that jibe. "If we could save some, and then plan together to take action—I don't know—just something. Some kind of action—not just waiting around to be driven like a flock of sheep. Something—you're a man. You ought to know what to do. I know something must be done, but I'm a woman, and I don't know what to plan."

Lennox turned to watch the violet, rose-veined mountains. "Protests don't do any good," he said at last.

"I'm not asking you to make protests. I'm asking you to do something, even if it is just to warn people, to tell them."

"And how?"

She stamped her foot like an angry child.

"Look, before nine o'clock the trucks will be moving out of the village. They'll have their 'volunteers' whether it's men or women and children. And along with the trucks will be that car with the two men who watched the Schichtl house today. You didn't know, did you, that two men were watching you all afternoon while the police were paying you a visit? These two men have talked about you. And they were talking about some airfield in Egypt. They were worried about that airfield—and they were talking about it when they were discussing you, so it has something to do with you."

"What airfield?" This time he was startled. The Germans had been holding a post-mortem on their failure as American airmen yesterday. And they weren't satisfied with it. Perhaps he had been too clever about that Beni Jara.

"One of them said they could find out about it from von Haller in Kastelruth."

"And who in creation is von Haller?"

"An expert on airfields. He arrives on the Schlern in the next few days. He is to plan something up here. That's all I know."

It was enough. It was news of several kinds. Lennox

stared at the girl's white face, with all its color and subtle shadows blotted out by the darkness, and then his lips tightened as he saw everything very clearly. It was a clever trick. She had been told enough to win his confidence. She was to appear as the girl, betrayed by her uncle, who wanted action against the Germans. And if he were to say, "But there is action being planned. Come along, we need women like you to help us,"—well, then, the Germans would have very quick, very final proof. It wouldn't only be Lennox who would be arrested and questioned. It would be Frau Schichtl who had sheltered him this winter, it would be the neighboring Kasals. It would be Mahlknecht and all his friends.

"Who else was talking about these things?"

"Only my uncle and these two men. They were asking him about you. You see, my uncle spent part of his time in the Zillertal when he was in the North Tyrol. He has friends there."

He stared at the darkened mountains. The alpine glow had ended. The peaks were now black shadows in a night sky. Torches were being lit around the garden of the Hotel Post. The dancing would soon begin now.

Eva Mussner seemed to sense the direction of his thoughts, for she gripped his arm. "What can we do?" she asked. "What can we do?"

"What *can* we do?" he repeated. "Don't be a fool asking unanswerable questions. You are only putting us all in danger."

She drew back quickly from him. "Then why did you let me talk? Why did you let me go on hoping that here was someone who would listen to me?"

"Look, I never let you go on hoping. Don't start inventing things." Additional things, he added to himself. "Besides, what can anyone do? We've no guns. Nothing. Bare hands against revolvers and machine guns, eh? And nothing would be solved. Violence would bring reprisal."

"You've no guns? Not one of you here has a gun?

You've all handed them over to the Germans like a batch of ninnies?"

He smiled and said, "We've no guns." Not handed over but hidden, and well-hidden for the day on which they would be needed.

"Why, even my uncle had more sense than that," she said. "He has a gun."

"Doesn't he trust his new friends? Or is he afraid of his old ones?" Lennox asked derisively. He began walking towards the garden of the Hotel Post.

Eva Mussner didn't follow him. He looked round in some surprise. He hadn't expected to be able to shake her off as suddenly as this. She was running towards the alley which led to the Mussner house. She was running home to her uncle, to tell him and his German friends that it was useless to try to find out anything from this Peter Schichtl, for there was obviously nothing to be found out.

Lennox should have been congratulating himself: he should have felt delighted. But somehow the feeling of satisfaction was tempered with bitterness. He had almost believed her. Somehow he was angry that anyone as lovely and intelligent as Eva Mussner had joined the Judas gang.

CHAPTER 20

The dancing was about to begin.

Lennox, on the fringe of the crowd, saw that no Germans had yet appeared. Eight o'clock that girl had said. That gave about fifteen minutes of grace. Before then he would be meeting Johann near the church. (It was just as well he hadn't complicated Johann's emotions about a plan which might not be used. Now the plan would have to be used.) And then he realized that he was preparing to act on what the Mussner girl had said, and his anger about her turned against himself. Bloody fool, he said to himself. Bloody fool. He knew she was a collaborationist of the worst kind—the kind that tries to trip up his own countrymen—and yet he had been thinking in terms of "eight o'clock," and of a German car with two potentially dangerous spies in it, racing to Kastelruth and the expert on airfields. He wished desperately that he could talk to the men at Schönau about this. They would know what to do. But the responsibility was his. He looked round at the people beside him. They felt some of the danger. They didn't know it all. The responsibility was all his.

The musicians, their energy restored by a hasty supper, were grouping together under a flowering chestnut tree. The red-faced man who was involved with the tuba tried a few muted blasts. There was a stirring among the people. Some of the younger women had taken off their hats. Lennox noted that their partners were only very young boys or fatherly men. They formed up in a long queue, with the first couple ready to climb up the three wooden steps to the dance platform and lead off the first measure. Lighter torches had been fixed in sockets on the wooden poles at each corner of the platform. The last curious child was pulled firmly down from his perch on the surrounding railing. The drummer was anxiously eying the concertina player.

Something wasn't quite in order. There was a stirring, a rustling, a murmur among the waiting pairs of dancers. They parted, either as if they were pushed aside or were avoiding someone. And then that someone was climbing the three steep steps, was standing alone on the wooden platform. It was Eva Mussner.

She gripped the railing's balustrade with one hand as if to steady herself. Her other hand was hidden under her apron. She said, with her clear voice carrying across the crowded garden out into the street where Lennox stood, "Go home at once. Leave here—now. The Germans are coming in a few minutes to gather men into their trucks. If they cannot find men they will take boys and women as hostages. Go. Show them that you are unwilling. Show them that if they do this to us then we know that they are worse than the Italians. Show them that if it is trouble they are seeking then they'll get it."

Lennox stood unmoving, rigid. Only his mind was active as his eyes watched.

Somewhere a man shouted. Shouted in anger. The crowd was silent. Their distrust of this girl left them doubting, hesitating. The man shouted again. It was Mussner himself, pushing his way to the platform. Two Germans in black uniform followed him. There was a stirring among the people, as if by the anger in these three men's faces they began to hesitate in their doubt. As Mussner leaped up the stairs and gripped his niece's shoulder they began to believe her words. Eva Mussner struggled against the strength of her uncle.

Lennox raised his voice and yelled. "Quick. Scatter into the darkness. Quick."

The Nazi policemen halted and turned to look in his direction. But the crowd was moving at last as if the authority of his shout at that moment had decided them. "Quick, Scatter," other voices were calling. "Quick; into the darkness."

The crowd increased its speed. It was pouring out of every side of the garden. Men and women and children hurried past Lennox as he stood jammed against the shadow of the inn wall. They were half running now, but there was no panic. For instance, a child stumbled and one of the fair-haired girls stooped to pick him up and then hurried on. The men were helping the older women. The first waves of people were already disappearing into the dark side roads which would lead them up into the woods. From the distance came the sound of trucks in low gear, pulling their way into the village.

"Here they come. Quick," Lennox yelled. The last doubtful stragglers broke into a run. The two Nazi policemen, unable to move in the surge of people, had grasped the man nearest them. Lennox saw the tuba player swing the large brass instrument, as if it were a battering ram, and knock the Germans sideways. And then the tuba player and the man he had freed were running towards him. Lennox himself started out of the safety of the shadows. He was halfway to the platform and Eva Mussner when the first shot rang out. It came from the platform. Eva Mussner had fired it.

Lennox saw Mussner crumple and fall, and he knew he could not help the girl now. The Nazi policemen were too quick to answer; their revolvers were drawn and they had fired at the platform. The last fringes of the crowd, now reaching the roadway, turned to stare back at the garden. They saw Eva Mussner falling to lie beside her uncle. One of the policemen fired again at the girl. But her body lay still. The last of the people at Hinterwald's feast day moved quickly away among the dark houses.

Lennox began running too. Behind him there were the shouts of the two Germans in civilian dress, of the other Nazi policemen. He caught up with the tuba player. Together, they raced out of the garden. The tuba player was cursing the Germans, over and over again. As they separated Lennox could still hear him, stumbling through the darkness, cursing the Germans.

Lennox, as he raced up a side path, saw two trucks arriving in the village street behind him. But the street was already emptied as the garden had been. The German soldiers were left to stare at the German policemen and the torches on the platform, at a tuba and scattered hats and a dropped shawl lying on the grass.

Lennox halted at the edge of a small belt of trees, and regained his sense of direction. He heard movements near him, but they weren't Germans. The officer in command had given no order for pursuit: he probably realized it was useless, with his men blundering about over strange ground in this darkness. Perhaps he even saw the ridiculousness of such pursuit. Its little chance of success only made the Germans more of a laughingstock. Lennox listened until he was almost certain he was right in his guess. That was the most he could allow himself. He couldn't go back to see. He had to reach Johann. They had a job to do. Now the job was more urgent than ever. If Eva Mussner's death was to be justified the job had to be done and done well.

As he made his way quickly towards the church Lennox kept thinking of the last moments in the hotel garden. At this moment he seemed to see it all more clearly than he had seen it then. It happened so quickly that his eyes hadn't believed. Eva Mussner had suddenly freed herself from her uncle's grasp, just as the two German spies had appeared. That was the moment she had chosen. Of that Lennox was convinced. She had waited until most of the people were gone, until the Germans could see her plainly.

And she had uncovered her right hand, which she had held stubbornly under her apron. She had a revolver, and she had fired it at Mussner. The Germans had taken no chances then. The man who fired that Lüger had been near enough to kill.

Lennox stared into the dark masses of shadows to the southwest of the church. The shrine of St. Johann was over there, but he couldn't see it. His eyes seemed still blinded by the flaring torches lighting an emptied garden and German faces turning towards the platform as they forgot the fleeing people. He still saw the heavy bulk of Mussner falling at the girl's feet, the sort of useless way she then held the revolver. He still saw the way she had fallen too as the German bullet retaliated. Flaring torches, an emptied square, and one collaborationist less to be killed. And a girl willing to die to prove to the Germans that she alone was guilty, to prove to her people that she was innocent.

"Here! Here!" The urgent whisper was Johann's. "What's wrong? What happened?"

Lennox regained his breath. "The people got away. Scattered. An alarm was given, but our plans stand. We have a job to do." He was beginning to see more clearly now in the shadow of the tree under which Johann had waited. "Where's the rope?"

"Sent it on ahead—special delivery. I felt we might have to make a quick dash. Besides, that rope's heavy. Too much like work carrying it." Johann started to move away from the village, traveling westward, following trees as far as they would shelter them.

"Whom did you send?" Lennox's voice was worried.

Johann grinned widely. "Don't worry, cousin. They can be trusted. They will arrive with the rope just about the time we reach the place."

They had better, Lennox thought grimly. He didn't even answer Johann's question about the shots from the village. "Later," he said impatiently. "Later—when we've finished

our job." He forced himself to keep up with Johann's quick
pace. If you didn't admit you were exhausted then you
weren't exhausted. He had failed Eva Mussner once: he
wasn't going to fail her a second time.

CHAPTER 21

There was nothing to do now but wait.

Lennox sat wearily beside the tree. Across the road from him Johann was sitting equally well hidden. He was worrying too, Lennox realized, although that cheery grin was still probably in place. For every now and again there would be a flick of movement to the darkened rope which stretched between them.

Lennox gave up wondering if the rope was strong enough, if windshield height would be the most effective, if the trees were well chosen to bear the strain. He looked at the dark road, twisting and curving down the hillside. At night, with no moon yet strong enough to light the rise and fall of ground, he could not be sure that this was the best place. He had to rely on Johann for this choice. He tried to reassure himself by looking at the bridge on his right. He could hear the strong fall of the torrent under it, and the noise of the rushing waters gave him at least an assurance of depths.

The steep hillside, falling away from the scattered trees on Johann's side of the road into a short precipice, had seemed abrupt and dangerous enough to him in the darkness. Yet, standing over there, looking down into sharp crags hidden by the night's blackness, he had wished he could have seen this part of the road by daylight. Or even by moonlight. Then he would know whether the rope, strung across this road obliquely—with Johann's tree in advance of his chosen one—would be a real weapon or just a simple-minded booby trap. Behind him was the hill-side down which he and Johann had slithered. Up there, to his left, were the two boys who had brought the rope to this place. They were keeping watch on the long curve of road descending from Hinterwald along this hillside towards Kastelruth. The boys were to let them know when the first headlights were approaching. They were to let them know whether it was a car's headlights or a truck's. Lennox had no interest any more in the trucks.

It was strange that when this plan had first formed in his head, as he had climbed down from Schönau this afternoon he had been thinking of merely stopping a truck. Just something to halt it to give those inside a chance to scatter over the hillside. Some might have escaped. It had struck him as funny, at that time, that he should have first come up to these mountains by planning his own escape, and that he should now be leaving them by planning escape for others. But now those others had escaped, not through him, but through a girl. She had been right in sensing that her people should be warned publicly and forced to make an open choice. Now those of them who had thought they could stay neutral, and still keep their independence, knew that there was no choice. After tonight and that girl's death there could be only those who were either anti-German or pro-German. She had forced the issue before the Germans could bewilder her people with smiles and false promises. She had been right, and he had been wrong. She was dead, and he was alive.

From the hillside above him he heard the noise of a dislodged stone. He was ready by the time the boy reached him. The hoarse, excited whisper said, "Headlights. Car first, traveling fast. Two trucks a mile behind, moving slowly."

"Right." Lennox flapped the rope sharply three times and felt an answering tug from Johann. They lifted the rope carefully, pulling it even and taut, and secured it tightly round their trees. Perhaps because of the wire woven into it, it did not feel as if it were sagging. Lennox was wondering whether the blotched coloring of the rope would show—patches of the stain had come off on the boys' hands and clothes as they carried it here—and then decided that perhaps these shadings would be better than a rope forming too much of a black line. Certainly, it didn't form a white line and it wasn't obvious to his eye at the moment. But headlights might pick it up, even if its oblique stretch would lessen that danger. All he could do now was to trust the curving road which made the headlights less effective. They ought to swing out over the ravine as the car came round that corner, and before they were focusing on the road properly the rope would be struck.

He hoped to God that Johann had moved away from the tree to his piece of chosen cover. If the car skidded it was likely to fall in his direction. This rope would only have halted a slow-moving truck. But a quickly moving car by its own speed would have more damage done to it. That was what they hoped for, anyway. Johann had insisted on taking that side of the road. He could, so he had solemnly sworn, hang onto a mountainside by his eyelashes if necessary.

The noise of rushing water had obliterated the sound of the car's approach. Lennox heard it just before he saw the headlights' yellow glare probing into the darkness. He had only time to flatten himself behind the tree. The grim sequence of noise was too confused, to quick, to be analyzed. The rope snapped, and whipped dangerously over his head back around the tree. We have failed, he thought desperately; failed, God damn us to everlasting hell. And then he heard only the sound of rushing water. He raised his head.

The car had swung around and was hanging on the edge of the road, its front wheels on the last foot of ground. The rope had shattered its windshield, and had been cut by the frame. The driver had lost control, and the road was torn where the wheels had skidded deeply into its surface.

Lennox couldn't be sure that the four men in the car were dead. They seemed lifeless—two, at least, were unpleasant to look at—but they might only be stunned and injured. For a moment he stood looking at the two men in civilian clothes who had watched from the Kasal barn, the two men who had made such amiable Allied airmen. The others in the car were the two policemen who had questioned him in the Schichtl house that afternoon. Well, here was a combination that would work no more together. Whatever they knew would never be written down as a report.

"Let's give it a push," Johann said urgently. "There's a good drop into the torrent."

Lennox was already reaching into the car, feeling for the reverse. Then it only needed a very short push indeed. The torrent was silenced as the car's wild plunge ended. Lennox backed slowly away from the edge of the precipice, his ears still shocked by the sudden smash after the tense moment of waiting. The torrent's voice lifted once more.

"Now your rope," Johann's practical voice said. He had already uncoiled the length from his tree. "We have less than two minutes."

The boy who had brought the warning of the car's approach was already unwinding the rope from the tree beside which Lennox had lain. The other boy had come down from his vantage point to see what had happened. He helped, too. The rope was uncoiled and laboriously unknotted. The two boys, carrying its folds between them, started over the hill.

"They know what to do with it. And with themselves. Come on, we had better not be found near here either." Johann's advice was good. Lennox followed him wearily, imitating Johann's bent shoulders and half-running pace. He would have liked to stay to see the trucks arrive, but it was safer to leave curiosity unsatisfied. The drivers must have heard the noise. They were probably traveling still more slowly, for they would now be expecting some kind of trouble. Then their lights would pick out the skid-marks on the road, for the surface had been badly torn. But even if they guessed that some accident had happened—a tire suddenly blown out or a turn too sharp and too quick—they could see little over that precipice edge. It was too steep, too deep, and the night was too dark. Later, when the moon came up, they would be able to see something. But there could be no salvage party until daylight.

Once they were over the spine of the hill Johann's pace slackened, and he walked upright. But even being able to move more naturally didn't lessen Lennox's exhaustion.

"I'm tired. I'm damned tired," he said to Johann. I'm out of training remember."

"Maybe," Johann said, without much conviction. "What happened in the village?"

"I'll tell you when we see your uncle. I need my breath for climbing. I suppose we are heading in his direction now?"

"Yes. We've got to report."

"At Schönau?"

"Yes. Good job you know how to cross the waterfall. It's tricky at night."

Lennox groaned. He had forgotten the waterfall.

"You'll manage it," Johann said cheerfully. "After tonight we could manage anything, couldn't we?"

Lennox wasn't so inclined to agree with that.

Anyway, he thought, there was one thing they had managed to do. The reports and suspicions which that car had been carrying to Kastelruth had been blotted out. Other reports would be made, other suspicions might grow, but these particular ones would do no more damage. That was one thing they had managed to do. They and Eva Mussner.

CHAPTER 22

Schönau—the beautiful high meadow—was earning its name. The sun was strong today, so Lennox had taken off his jacket and opened the collarless neck of his shirt. He stretched his body contentedly on the carpet of fine green grass. There were more flowers spreading their miniature petals close to the ground. The scent of pine and new-leaved trees from the surrounding woods was stronger. Each day there was a little more of the promise of summer.

Lennox stopped looking at the blue sky with its soft white clouds, high and unmoving over the line of mountaintops, and turned to watch the foresters' hut. No one had come out yet. Either they were giving him plenty of time to make up his mind, or they were discussing some new points. Not that he could imagine them finding a new point: since he and Johann had arrived here last night, there had been enough careful discussion to fill a millpond.

It was the American who came out at last from the hut and walked casually towards Lennox. Nothing in his leisurely step—he was a loose-limber sort of chap with easy movements—nothing in his placid face showed he was coming here with a purpose.

Lennox rose to his feet. . . . Private Lennox, sir, reporting. . . .

"Cut that out," Thomson said, with his good-natured smile. He dropped into the grass, and motioned Lennox to sit beside him. "You'd better be careful," he warned, "or we'll commission you temporarily on the field."

"I'd prefer to remain as I am," Lennox said.

"Determined guy, aren't you? But you've certainly been more co-operative than we expected."

"Thank you," Lennox said. He half smiled, and he suddenly thought of the colonel. Not co-operative . . . was that the colonel's description of him? Anyone seemed not co-operative when he was asked to do what he didn't want to do. Especially if his mind had been quite made up otherwise. "I suppose I was a sort of resentful blighter," he added, his smile broadening.

"You probably only needed a rest up here in these mountains. They'd cure anyone."

Lennox nodded. "I didn't know I was cured either. That's the funny thing. I didn't know it, until the two Jerries dressed as American airmen walked into the Schichtl kitchen. I had been telling myself all winter that I was a useless crock—" Lennox halted in embarrassment. He was saying too much. The American was so easy to talk to. He just sat there, with his arms around his knees and a friendly grin on his face. Not too much of a grin, either, but just enough to make you go on talking. Lennox went on. "There didn't seem anything I could do up here. You fellows were coming, and I was only a stopgap. There didn't even seem much for me to do if I ever managed that escape to the south. The Army would probably discharge me. This hand has been getting worse all winter. A prison camp wasn't the best place to cure it properly."

"Tough luck," Thomson agreed. "But I've heard of left-handers who were crack shots. Don't see why you couldn't learn. Besides, this war won't last forever. You'll be thinking of going back to your old job then, and it won't matter a damn whether you can shoot a gun or not."

Lennox was silent.

"Will it?" the American asked sympathetically.

"No. I don't suppose it will." His voice had changed, and the American watched him curiously. If the American had lost eight years of his life, Lennox thought, he wouldn't

be so puzzled. Eight years learning to paint, scraping up
money for tuition, living from hand to mouth so that he
could get abroad where the light was warm and the colors
were bright. There had been trouble with his people because he wouldn't settle down to a profession. There had
been a lot of private trouble and disappointments because
he had insisted on going on with his painting. And then,
after eight years, there had been the beginning of some
success. That was the summer of 1939. Eight years . . .
eight years, hell! He wasn't the only chap who was now
finding that after this war he would have to start all over
again.

"Have you made your decision?" Thomson asked. "Do
you take your long-promised trip south, or do you go into
North Tyrol with Johann?"

"It's a long walk either way." Lennox's voice was quite
normal now. "I'll travel north with Johann."

"Fine." Thomson was genuinely pleased, perhaps even
relieved. He rose. "Come on. They're waiting for us in
the hut."

As they walked slowly over the broad meadow the
American said, "Lennox, I should be keeping my mouth
shut, but I won't. If you traveled south there might be still
hope for your hand. If you go north—well, you could
get no specialist's treatment there. You realize that?"

"Yes. I'll just have to make my left hand useful," Lennox said. And if I lose that one, he thought, I'm damned
if I don't learn to paint with my toes. He began to smile.

"We are about ready to push off," Thomson said.
"We've been given two of those guides you were talking
about. You and Johann will leave tonight. Schroffenegger's
son is going along with you."

Lennox nodded "Is Johann still asleep?"

"Yes, he's earned it."

And that was true. For last night Johann had gone back
to the village to scout carefully around. He had returned
at dawn with a variety of news. The people had left the

hillside, some to reach their distant houses, other to return to the village. They knew grimly that there had only been a respite and no material gain for them. Even now the Germans would be planning a change of policy towards their Austrian "cousins." But there had been a moral victory for Eva Mussner. It was the girl's death which had shocked the people most of all. They had been angered by the fact that the Germans had chosen their feast day in order to gather a rich haul of what they would call volunteers. But it was the girl's death they were talking about. Mussner's treachery and the danger to the village coming from all such treachery, had been clearly shown in that last scene in the garden. Those who had witnessed it were describing it in detail to those who had already fled. They told how the girl had stood with her uncle's revolver, no longer pointing, no longer threatening. Yet the Germans had killed her. And she had not shot her uncle as a murderess would have killed, out of envy or greed or evil. Yet the Germans had killed her. Without a trial. From now on, Johann had reported, there were no more neutrals in this district. Mahlknecht's list of those who were doubtful friends of the Allied cause, because they were neutral, could now be scrapped.

"He's earned it," repeated Thomson. "By the way, we got some more news when you were asleep this morning. The Fifth is rolling up the Krauts like a red carpet. The Eighth is slugging right up the middle of Italy. I'll lay you five to one we'll be in Rome within the month."

Lennox shared the American's wide smile for a moment. "No takers," he said. "I'm on your side." He turned to stare at the mountain peaks to the south. He had stopped walking.

"Wish you were with them?" Thomson asked. "So do I. And yet we are, in a kind of a way. We're an advance unit. That's us."

When Lennox didn't answer he asked quietly, "What made you choose to go into the North Tyrol with Johann?

You'll be useful there. We need you. But why did you choose it?"

The American would never have got his answer if he hadn't been so easy to talk to. If Shaw had asked that question Lennox would have said, "It's a nice climate, I hear." But to Thomson he said, "I'm trying to show some-one I'm not just the selfish fool she thought I was."

"Hope she appreciates that some day," Thomson said. He looked as if he wanted to ask more, but he didn't. It was just as well. Lennox couldn't have answered that one. He couldn't have answered, "She is dead. She was shot by the Germans."

In embarrassment he said quickly, "I'll do more damage to Jerry up there than I could from a hospital behind our lines."

Thomson was satisfied. Lennox suddenly felt satisfied too.

In the hut there were Mahlknecht and Shaw and young Josef Schroffenegger. Johann was snoring steadily on one of the straw mattresses. He could sleep until dusk came. And then he and Lennox and young Josef would set out together. They would climb to the mountain hut near the top of the peak on their journey. They should reach there before midnight, and sleep there, and leave there—to tackle the difficult part of crossing a mountain—in the good light of early morning.

On the bunk next to the one where Johann lay there was the equipment they would need, and the small packages of food which they could carry. Schroffenegger's son had brought these necessary supplies this morning. He would be useful on this trip. Both he and Johann had climbed through that sea of mountains once before. Then it had been to avoid Italian recruitment for the Albanian campaign. Now it was to win recruits for the fight against Germany.

"He's going," Thomson said to Shaw, and they both looked satisfied.

Mahlknecht too was in good spirits. The plans were well made. They had purpose, careful arrangement, and more than a chance of success. The months of worry were over: action lay ahead. He laid his hand on Lennox's shoulder. "I didn't kidnap you this time, did I?" he asked jokingly. And yet he was anxious, too, as if he wanted reassurance that Lennox no longer thought of him as a whipcracker.

Lennox said, "So it was you who insisted on giving me time to decide?" His voice and his smile showed that resentment was dead.

Mahlknecht laughed. "Last time I had no choice. It was you, or nothing. And it did some good, didn't it?" He nodded towards Thomson and Shaw. "They wouldn't be here unless you had come up onto the Schlern."

"Oh, perhaps they would," Lennox said, but he was pleased that Mahlknecht had spoken that way.

A birdcall came from the path which Schroffenegger's second son guarded.

"It's a friend," Mahlknecht said, in answer to the three foreigners' tension. "That's the signal for a friend."

"Better keep him out of here even if he is a friend," Shaw said crisply.

Mahlknecht nodded and stepped outside.

After a few minutes he returned with a bundle. "More food," he said. "It's Katharina. She wants to see you, Peter."

"Was it wise of her to come here?" Shaw asked sharply. Thomson too was looking worried.

"My sister sent her. Katharina says no one followed her. There are only four policemen at the Golden Roof Inn now, and they've stayed there all day. Perhaps they are waiting for instructions, or perhaps they feel they need reinforcements. The village is in an ugly mood. My sister thought it was safe, and I think we can trust her. She has sent a specially marked map which her husband made when he was a guide, and some more food, and some brandy."

"All right," Shaw said. "But send the girl away quickly." He offered no further objections.

"She has a message for you, Peter," Mahlknecht repeated.

Lennox walked to the door, very conscious of the look in both the officers' eyes.

"Business and pleasure mixed?" Thomson was saying with a laugh. "We could learn a tip or two from him, Roy." But in the joke there was a neatly conveyed piece of advice.

Katharina was waiting down near the path into the wood. She held a neat package in her clasped hands. Her cheeks were flushed, her eyes smiled as she watched him approach.

"Frau Schichtl sent me with this. She said you needed it." She held out the small package with the same directness in her movement as in her words.

It contained a small pad of paper, something which he could slip into his jacket pocket easily. And his two favorite pencils. And some of the sheets of paper which had lain in his bedroom: the first attempts to sketch with his left hand were there, along with the drawings he had made last week. Frau Schichtl was telling him that if he could make so much progress he could make still more. He had thought she had never paid much attention to his scribbling, but in her quiet undemonstrative way she had known all the time.

Katharina looked at the contents of the package with disappointment. "Is that all?" she asked. And then she noticed Lennox's face. Something had pleased him. Something had made him happy. So she smiled too.

"Frau Schichtl tells me that you are going into the mountains for the summer, like all the younger men." She nodded in the direction of the Schlern peaks.

"Yes," he answered. Obviously the girl knew nothing about the mission into the North Tyrol. And he was not leaving for just this summer, either. The job he had to do now would last through the autumn, perhaps even into the winter as well. It might be spring before he saw Hinterwald again. With luck. . . .

She gave him her hand and said, "I wish you a safe journey, and a quick return."

"Thank you." He was equally grave.

She turned to go back along the path which would take her to the waterfall. And then she halted and said in dismay, "I nearly forgot. . . . Frau Schichtl gave me a message for you. After the war is over the church walls will need a man who can paint."

When he didn't reply Katharina said, "That was the message. It sounds silly, I know. But that was what she said."

"It isn't at all silly. It makes a lot of sense." He smiled and added, "I shan't forget that invitation. Tell Frau Schichtl that."

He stood watching the girl as she walked away with that long, even stride. She looked back and waved as she reached the curve in the path. She hesitated for a moment, and he knew how she would be smiling. Then the gold-braided head was hidden by the green trees.

Lennox moved towards the hut. He walked with a lighter step. In the spring, he thought once more, and then he laughed. For he knew he was indeed cured. He had stopped brooding about the past: the long, bitter wasted months and years had lost their power to nag him. And now they didn't even seem so wasted; he might find that they had taught him something if only he were willing to learn. Anyway, he was cured. He could think of the future.

Back in the hut Thomson and Shaw were showing signs of impatience. Mahlknecht and young Schroffenegger were talking quietly together. "Is this the way you always work?"

Shaw said with a slightly raised eyebrow, and an acid
smile.

"She's on the young side, if you ask me," was Thomson's milder reproof.

Lennox laughed. "Don't be bloody fools," he said, and
he didn't even remember their rank. "Now, what are these
final instructions?"

His whole manner was so different, so confident and
alert and interested, that the two officers exchanged
glances. Their annoyance left them. Shaw, who had been
on the point of deciding that Lennox might be too erratic
and undecided a man for this North Tyrol job, was thankful he had kept his mouth shut. Plans depended on the
men who carried them out. It was better to have a plan
incomplete and a man who was sure of himself, than to
have an excellent plan and a man who was unsettled.

"Good," he said, most emphatically, and motioned Lennox to sit down at the rough wooden table and look at
the outspread map as they talked.

When Johann woke the hut was in darkness, and the
Englishman and the American had already gone. Young
Josef Schroffenegger was sitting with Paul Mahlknecht. and
they were talking together in the quiet, slurred drawl of
men discussing important things. Johann stretched and
yawned. "That was good," he said with satisfaction. "I
could travel for days now. Where's Peter?"

"Outside. He's waiting for you to wake up. He's getting
impatient." There was a pleased note in his uncle's voice
which wakened Johann still more.

"So?" he said, and went out-of-doors. Some cold water
from the spring at the side of the hut would freshen him
up. He was fully awake by the time he had dashed the icy
water over his face and neck. He couldn't see Lennox at
first, and then he noticed—as his quick eye scanned the
trees which encircled the meadow—that the Britisher was

sitting on the ground as motionless as the log lying beside him.

Johann crossed over towards him. Lennox was watching the alpine glow.

"All set," Johann asked.

"All set," Lennox said, but he didn't take his eyes from the living mountains.

"Pretty, eh?" Johann said, with the inadequacy of well-concealed pride. "Haven't you got accustomed to these fireworks by this time?"

Lennox laughed, and rose to his feet.

"Where do we go, Johann?" he asked.

Johann pointed towards a wall of gold and ruby and amethyst. "Up over there," he said, "that's the way. It's easier than it looks. We'll manage it."

"I'll make a damned good try, anyway."

"We'll manage it," Johann's voice was hard. They began walking towards the hut. "We'll beat them. They asked for it. They'll get it." At the door of the hut he said, "I've been thinking. I've been wondering just how many girls they have murdered in all these years?" Lennox didn't answer: no one knew the answer to that.

The table was lighted by one small piece of candle. The windows were shuttered, the door was carefully closed. Mahlknecht and young Schroffenegger were examining the equipment and clothes for the journey. The food and brandy which Katharina had brought were laid out on the table. Everything was arranged: everything had been taken care of. All that the three young men had to do now was to remember their very complete directions. There were two addresses in the North Tyrol which were reliable—Thomson and Shaw had vouched for that—and they could make these their headquarters. For at these addresses they would find men who had radio contact with London. Shaw's last instructions had been, "If you want to send news here then send it to London. They will see that

Thomson gets it. Our news to you will travel the same way."

Lennox pulled on an extra pair of heavy woolen socks, with their heels well soaped. He laced his climbing boots carefully: they must give support without being tight. Johann was packing what they needed for the journey into a rucksack. Each of them carried a sheathed knife, and each had been given a revolver.

"Well," Mahlknecht said, standing beside Lennox and watching him tie the last lace into a firm double knot, "well, you will be back here by next spring at the latest. Perhaps sooner, but . . ." He shrugged his shoulders. Nothing was certain in war. Time drags out longer than one expects.

Lennox rose and tested the comfort of his boots and the thick layer of socks by tramping on the earth floor. He picked up the light *loden* cape which would protect him from wind and rain, and slung it over his shoulders. He followed Johann and young Josef, who were moving towards the door. Johann gave his uncle the usual forefinger salute, but tonight his lips were solemn and his eyes were grave.

Lennox looked back at Paul Mahlknecht standing alone in the empty room.

"I'll be here next spring," he replied. "Perhaps a lot of us will be here before then," he said.

Paul Mahlknecht must have been thinking along these same lines, for there was a sudden smile in the dark, thoughtful eyes.

"Perhaps," Mahlknecht said. His voice was very quiet as he added, "We shall be waiting."

Peter Lennox closed the door. He followed the others into the dark night.